Red Light in the Pyrenees

Elly Grant

Red Light in the Pyrenees
By Elly Grant

Published by Author Way Limited through
CreateSpace
Copyright 2012 Elly Grant

This book has been brought to you by -

Author Way

Book cover designed by Chris Carlisle
Discover other Author Way Limited titles at -
http://www.authorway.net
Or to contact the author mailto:ellygrant@authorway.net

Red Light in the Pyrenees is a work of fiction written by Elly Grant. No characters or events in the book are real and any similarity to people and events living or dead is purely coincidental. .All rights reserved.

ISBN: 1484896165
ISBN-13: 978-1484896167

ACKNOWLEDGMENTS

For my husband and my children

and with thanks to Author Way, Amazon
and CreateSpace for making it happen
.

Elly Grant

CHAPTER 1

The body of Madame Henriette is lying through the broken window of the kitchen door with the lower part of the frame supporting her lifeless corpse. Her head, shoulder and one arm hang outside, while the rest of her remains inside, as if she has endeavoured to fly, Superman style, through the window and become stuck. She is slumped, slightly bent at the knees, but with both feet still touching the floor. Her body is surrounded by jagged shards of broken glass.

From the kitchen this is all one sees. It is not until you open the window to the side of the door and look through it, that you see the blood. Indeed quite a large area of the tiny courtyard has been spattered with gore as Madame Henriette's life has pumped out of her. One shard has sliced through her throat and by the amount of blood around, it seems to have severed her jugular. She must have been rendered unconscious almost immediately as she has made no effort to lift herself off the dagger-like pieces of glass which are sticking out from the frame.

There is blood on the pot plants and on the flowering creeper which grows up the wall, dividing this house from the neighbour's. It has also sprayed the small, hand crafted, wrought iron table and chairs. The blood is beginning to turn black in the morning sun and there's a sizeable puddle congealing on the ground under the body. This will need to be spread with sawdust when the clean up begins, I think to myself.

There is rather a lot of blood on Madame Henriette's head as it has run down her face from the gaping wound on her throat, but it's still possible to see that her hair is well-styled and her face is fully made up. Her clothes are tight and rather too sexy for a woman of her age and her push-up bra and fish-net stockings seem inappropriate at this time of the morning. If you didn't know any better, you would assume that Madame Henriette is simply a lady of growing years trying desperately to hold on to her youth, but to her neighbours and those of us who have had dealings with her, the truth is much less forgiving. Madame Henriette is indeed a Madame. She is a lady of the night, a peddler of prostitutes, and this building which she owns is a brothel.

The house of Madame Henriette is situated in the old part of town where the cobbled streets are so narrow that only one car may pass at a time. All the buildings are tall and slim and made of stone. Each is distinguished from the next by different coloured shutters and different degrees of weathering to the facade.

When entering this house one would pass through a small door which is cut in a much larger, heavier one. The magnificent carved entrance looks overdressed in this street and harks back to a time when this area was much grander. Nowadays everyone wants modern and the town has spread out with alarming speed from this central point. The wealthy live in the suburbs. They have gardens, swimming pools and pizza ovens. From once being uptown and chic, these streets have become dreary and they now contain a lower class of citizen. They are a melting pot of students, foreigners and people who survive on state benefits. Sometimes holidaymakers rent here thinking the area is quaint and having the desire to experience a 'typical' French house in a 'typical' French street.

After entering through the door, which is immediately off the road, you would find yourself in a narrow hallway with a magnificent, old and ornate, tiled floor. A curved stone stairway with an iron banister rail then takes you to the upper floors. On the first floor, if you turned to your right, you would find yourself in the sitting room where Madame Henriette offered her guests some wine as they waited for one of her 'nieces' to fetch them. Then they would be taken to one of the bedrooms which are situated on the upper floors. To the left is the kitchen but few meals were cooked there. Food was usually very quickly thrown together from a selection of cold meats, cheese and bread, then hastily eaten by the girls as they grabbed a few spare moments between clients. All, of course, was washed down with glasses of heavy, red, cheap, local wine. The wine made both the food and the clients more palatable.

The body of Madame Henriette was discovered by her maid Eva who is a rather scrawny girl aged about twenty. She has mousy brown hair and grubby looking skin peppered with acne scars. Every day Eva came to work for Madame, her duties being to wash the sheets, clean the house and bring in the food from the market. She was also responsible for buying condoms and checking that each bedroom had a plentiful supply. Madame Henriette was fastidious about health and safety and would never allow sexual contact without condoms.

On discovering the body of her mistress, the shocked young woman fled the house and ran screaming into the street. One of the neighbours heard the screams and chose, on this occasion, not to ignore the noises coming from the vicinity of the house but instead telephoned for the emergency services and this is where my story begins.

CHAPTER 2

Some of you have met me before and you are aware that my name is Danielle and I am a police officer living and working in the Eastern Pyrenees in Southern France. It has been over two years since we first encountered one another and I can tell you, with some pride, that I now have jurisdiction over a large area stretching from south of Perpignan to the Spanish border. My recent success in handling serious crimes has ensured my quick promotion. Consequently, I am now called in to be the lead officer in all the major crime cases which occur in my area.

My best friend Patricia and I are still living in our little house on the outskirts of the small town where I was born. Although we will never meet with blanket approval, most people in the town now accept that two women can live together without the relationship being sexual, even if one of those women is a lesbian. Please don't misunderstand, Patricia and I love each other and sometimes we even sleep in the same bed, but that is as far as it goes. We are friends, loving friends, nothing more and nothing less.

Patricia and I have experienced remarkable changes in our lives over the last two years. I have advanced from being nothing more than a traffic cop to the esteemed position I now hold. Patricia has progressed from being an assistant in a funeral parlour to having her own business making and selling pies, pickles and jams. She has also established herself as an artist.

I am very proud of our achievements, and rightly so, as it was an uphill struggle. The hardest thing to gain was the acceptance of local people. The turning point for Patricia came when the wife of the Mayor befriended her and the Commune Committee commissioned a painting from her. It is difficult being a lesbian in a small town but easier if you have powerful friends. For me the turning point came with my handling of two major cases involving violent death and drugs. This led me to be considered a kind of saviour in my town.

I am eating breakfast in the kitchen when the call comes in about Madame Henriette. Ollee our dog is making a nuisance of himself because he wants some of the cheese I'm eating. How can I refuse this odd looking bundle of mischief when he is trying so hard to impress me? I cannot deny him, so most of my cheese ends up in his belly instead of mine. Although it's early on a Saturday morning, Patricia already has pans of apricots bubbling on the stove. She's trying to finish the task of making her jam before the day and the kitchen becomes too hot. Every so often Patricia checks the pans then goes back to the painting she's working on for a gallery in Perpignan.

"Must you go to work today?" she asks. "I was hoping we could go to the market in Ceret because I want to get a ham from Monsieur Charles. The one we have is almost finished and his are the best in the region. I've arranged to exchange six pots of pickles and three fruit pies for one of the really big ones."

"I've been called to Ceret for this job and I must go now," I reply. "I don't have time to wait for you, but if you put the jars and pies in my car you can meet up with me later. I'll be parking in the car park behind the main square and I'll give you my spare car key so you can get your stuff out of the boot when you need it. That way you and Ollee can travel in on the bus whenever you're ready."

"That's great Danielle," she replies. "Perhaps you won't be too long and we'll be able to have lunch in that stylish little place in the square."

"Perhaps," I reply. "We'll see."

The truth is I've been told to expect lots of blood so I might not be feeling like eating any lunch, stylish, or otherwise. When my colleague Raymond called from Ceret he said it was like a scene from a slasher movie, but I think he's probably exaggerating. Raymond is quite new to the job. He's never attended a violent death before, but he's assured me that he's up to the work. He also told me, rather proudly, that he didn't chuck up when he saw the corpse. Just as well because we can't have him contaminating the crime scene. I am to meet Raymond at the scene and a doctor has been summoned to examine the corpse before it can be moved. I have requested that my old friend Dr Poullet attends because we are used to working together, and besides, why not give my friend the work and the fee. Being the senior officer does have certain advantages.

Last year I would have been rushing out of the

door and racing to attend the scene, but now I take my time, because now I have the experience to know that the corpse is going nowhere and everyone must wait for me. So I finish my coffee, kiss Patricia on the cheek and pat Ollee on the head, before heading out of the door. I am excited to be attending another major incident because I'm making rather a good name for myself out of the death and destruction of others. I have no qualms about this because it's a reasonable assumption that for one person to succeed another must fail.

CHAPTER 3

As I drive towards Ceret the sun shines brightly through the car windows and I blink at the brilliant colours that surround me. The sky is a vivid blue and the trees on the mountains are a dozen, improbable shades of green. As I pass by the orchards the fruit trees are laden with golden peaches and apricots which make the air smell sweet and I feel very fortunate to live in this place. The grandeur and beauty of the mountains always humbles me and I wish I was going to the market with Patricia instead of to the bloodbath that awaits me in town.

Although it is still rather early in the day the car park is already full when I arrive in Ceret but I manage to squeeze my car onto a footpath where I abandon it. I place a sign on the windscreen to inform everyone that there is a police emergency, and this is an official car, just in case an over zealous officer has me towed away. Then I make my way to the house of Madame Henriette.

Raymond has cordoned off the whole street with tape to stop vehicles from driving along it, not that it makes much difference, as few cars travel this way. People who need access to their homes are ducking under the tape but they don't stop outside the house of Madame Henriette. Respectable people never stopped outside this house because everyone knew what went on inside and feared being found guilty by association.

When I enter the front door I am handed a white suit by a junior police officer.

"Is this so I don't contaminate the crime scene?" I ask.

"No Madame," he replies. "Raymond thought it would stop you getting blood on your uniform. These overalls were left over after the office was painted."

"I see you had a large budget," I say sarcastically as I tear the sleeve of the flimsy suit while trying to pull it over my uniform, but my humour is lost on him.

I ascend the stairs and enter the small kitchen where Raymond and a rather grumpy Dr Poullet are waiting.

"I hope you enjoyed your breakfast Danielle. I haven't even had a cup of coffee yet," Dr Poullet grumbles. "Some of us believed this to be an emergency and we have been waiting for you for forty minutes."

"Bonjour to you too, Dr Poullet," I reply.

"Hmph," is his response.

"Parking is impossible," I offer by way of an excuse.

"It was not impossible forty minutes ago, I had no problem," he replies gruffly.

I send the junior officer to fetch us all coffees and Poullet cheers up when I point out that he can charge double his fee for working at the weekend. The crime scene is indeed quite gruesome and Raymond and I stand well back as the doctor runs through his observations for me.

"It is most probably an accident," he says. "I think it likely she tripped over the chair which is overturned then put out her hand to try to stop herself from falling. I assume that's the reason her body is partly inside and partly outside the broken window and why she is suspended on the window frame. Rather undignified but so was her life," he observes. "She made no attempt to move so she probably lost consciousness very quickly through shock and blood loss."

"Is there any chance her death could have been caused by something other than an accident?" Raymond asks.

"Why do you ask?" I question. "Is there something I should know?"

"I'm not sure," he replies. "I have my suspicions that Madame Henriette was making money from more than just her girls. There have been mutterings about blackmail."

"Then perhaps you should investigate further," Dr Poullet says. "It doesn't change the cause of death. She died from blood loss and shock. I cannot completely rule out foul play but I'm pretty sure her death is simply the result of a ghastly accident."

I'm sorry Raymond has opened his mouth and voiced his opinions because now I'll have to look for further information. It would have been so much easier to accept Dr Poullet's explanation. Now I'll have to go through the motions of trying to find Madame Henriette's clients and neither they, nor their families, will be happy about that. Besides, who will care that some old whore is dead? Most people in this town will rejoice at the news.

I give Raymond instructions about how to arrange for the body to be removed and the house cleaned up. I inform him that I'll search for Madame Henriette's client book before I leave then I make my way upstairs to her bedroom. I expect her room to be all satin and silk and I'm quite disappointed to find it very ordinary and indeed rather shabby. I don't find a client book but I do remove her diary in case there are any clues amongst her jottings. When I make my way back downstairs I meet Dr Poullet at the front door.

"I'm claiming for the whole weekend because I'll have to do my report tomorrow," he says. "I trust you have no objections."

"None at all," I reply.

He holds his chin in his hand and narrows his eyes as if deep in thought, "Perhaps it might take me until Monday morning," he speculates, raising his bushy eyebrows.

"Maybe it will take you most of the day on Monday," I reply and I smile and nod at him.

"I would like to order some jam and pickles from Patricia," he says. "Perhaps an assortment of your choice, say six jars."

"I think you should make it ten," I reply. "You won't be disappointed, they're superb."

He offers me his hand and I shake it. "You will have my report by close of business on Monday. You will also have my bill."

"You will have the jam and pickles by close of

business on Monday. You will also have Patricia's bill," I reply with a smile. "It's a pleasure to do business with you," I add.

With the deal struck, we step out of the door and each of us goes our separate way. I think we're both relieved to be out of that house and back into the land of the living.

CHAPTER 4

I make my way through the busy streets with some difficulty because, as it is the height of summer and a beautiful sunny day, the town is alive with people. I spy Patricia about half way down a line of stalls and I am amazed that I've found her so easily in such a large crowd. Ollee sees me and he hurtles towards me through the legs of tourists and townsfolk yipping and yapping and leaping excitedly. Patricia throws her head back and laughs delightedly at the dog's antics then our eyes meet and she waves at me and signals for me to join her.

She is talking to Monsieur Charles and her hand is resting on the biggest ham on his stall. Monsieur Charles is over six feet tall with strong shoulders. His head is completely bald, as it has been since he was a young man. To compensate for the lack of hair on his head he has grown a magnificent handle bar moustache. He has very bushy eyebrows and a way of narrowing his eyes and smiling when he is thinking that gives him the look of a nineteenth century villain from an old movie.

"Isn't this the most wonderful ham?" Patricia says as I approach.

"It was a fair exchange," Monsieur Charles replies shyly. "Hello, Danielle," he continues, "Nasty business at the whorehouse, very nasty business."

"Yes," I reply. "Not the most pleasant way to

start a morning."

"I take it she's dead," he asks, "Accident was it?"

"I shouldn't really discuss the case but it would seem so," I reply.

Monsieur Charles gives an audible sigh and I wonder how many other men will be relieved.

"Monsieur Charles was just telling me about the lottery win," Patricia says changing the subject. "Someone from this region has won two hundred thousand euros in last week's draw, but they haven't come forward to claim it yet. It could be anyone. It might be someone we know," she speculates.

"We'll probably never know who it is as they'll wish to remain anonymous," Monsieur Charles says. "I know if I won the lottery I would definitely remain anonymous because, if my wife or my daughters found out, I would never see any of the money," he adds with a wry smile.

To say that Monsieur Charles is henpecked is an understatement because this gentle, kind man is completely under the thumb of his bossy wife. Madame Charles is on every committee and is deeply involved with the church. Very pious people always make me feel rather uncomfortable and Madame Charles is no exception. Something about her reminds me of my overbearing mother and I'm sure she must be very difficult to live with. Perhaps that's why Monsieur Charles is interested in news about Madame Henriette, I speculate.

"I would buy more chickens and an apricot

orchard and I would take Danielle on a little holiday. We've not had a holiday and we've been living in our house for two years now. I would get Ollee the biggest bone in the boucherie and a box full of new toys."

Patricia is already dreaming about spending the money that she has not won.

Monsieur Charles nods at Patricia then looks at me and laughs, "If only my family's desires were so simple," he says. "My wife and daughters would want designer this and designer that and bling bling here and bling bling there and I would have to work twice the hours to pay for it. It is better that I don't win. I will be a richer man for not winning."

"Perhaps the ticket was sold by our newsagent," Patricia speculates. "If so, Therese who works there might know the identity of the winner. It's a real mystery but quite exciting isn't it?"

"Patricia, Darling, it could have been bought anywhere in the region. One of the supermarkets could have sold the ticket. It may have been a lucky dip and the purchaser might not even have checked the numbers yet. Anything is possible. The only thing we know for certain is that none of us has won."

"Oh well," she replies, "We might not be rich but at least we're not poor. Help me to carry this monster of a ham to your car and then I'll buy you lunch."

"Now you're talking. I'm beginning to feel really hungry and, if we're quick, we'll get a table at the bistro before the place fills up with tourists."

We say goodbye to Monsieur Charles, then I

carry the ham as one would carry a small child and I think it weighs about the same, as we make our way through the throngs of people to the car. When we return to the square and are seated at a table outside the restaurant my thoughts return to one of the items on Patricia's wish list.

"Would you like to go for a holiday?" I ask her. "We could easily afford a few days away. Where would you like to go?"

"I don't really need a holiday, Danielle, but it would be nice," she says. "You've been working very long hours because of your promoted post. Now that things have settled down a bit, I think you could do with a change of scene. But I suppose, with this latest incident, it will be out of the question for a few weeks."

"I love my work and my position so I don't feel under any strain but I think it would do us both good to get a break and besides, we can afford it," I add. "So where would you like to go?"

"Whale watching in Alaska," she replies, quick as a flash.

"W-what," I stammer.

"Got ya," she says laughing, "Barcelona would be good."

CHAPTER 5

True to his word Dr Poullet's report arrives on my desk late on Monday afternoon and there are no surprises in it. I'm hopeful this will be the end of the matter, but when I arrive in the office on Tuesday, I'm told Monsieur Rene Charles has called and he would like me to phone him back regarding the Madame Henriette case. My colleague who took the call says that Monsieur Charles insisted on speaking to me, and only me, so he has no information to pass on. I feel an uncomfortable prickling on my skin, my instincts tell me that I might be about to open Pandora's box.

Although Monsieur Charles lives in Ceret, we arrange to meet in my office as he doesn't want anyone to see him talking to me. I agree to have my lunch late so he can come to the office while his wife is at the hairdresser's. I'm now pretty sure that Monsieur Charles has had dealings with Madame Henriette and he's obviously worried about it. Why else would he want to talk to me, of all people, unless he was afraid of being found out about something that he'd rather have kept to himself?

I'm concentrating deeply on a case, and I've read the same paragraph on my computer screen several times, when my intercom buzzer goes to announce the arrival of Monsieur Charles. I go to the outer office where I see him standing rather stooped, his head bowed, his eyes staring at his feet. He has his hands in his pockets and a paper package tucked under his arm. I close my office door behind me and the noise makes him look up.

"Bonjour, Monsieur Charles," I say. Turning to re-open the door I usher him inside.

"Please call me Rene," he says and he sits in the chair that I offer.

He places a rather pungent smelling, greasy, paper bag on the desk in front of me.

"Some Catalan sausage," he explains. "For you and Patricia, it's very good."

"That's very kind of you," I reply, touched by the gift. "Would you like some coffee? I'm just going to pour myself some."

"Thank you, yes," he answers.

I pour the coffees and place his in front of him and he lifts it and holds it in cupped hands. We sit sipping the coffees and I wait for him to speak but he is obviously finding it difficult to begin because he squirms in the seat like an embarrassed teenager.

"You have something you wish to discuss, Rene?" I ask, trying to nudge him along, "Something about the death of Madame Henriette perhaps?"

"Ah, yes, Hortense," he says, "Hortense Henriette. I knew her well. We went to school together but my parents didn't approve of her mother so we were never allowed to be friends. Her mother was also a whore but I liked her because I was a shy boy and she always took the time to talk to me. Hortense was the first girl, I ...... You know."

His voice tails off and his face burns with

shame.

"We were both fifteen and I thought she loved me until she asked for my pocket money. She said it was for condoms and I believed her. Until my friend Patrice told me that many of the boys in my year were paying for condoms too. It didn't stop me from liking her. So you see I couldn't have done her any harm."

"Why should I suspect you of hurting her?" I ask.

He studies my face for a moment then rubs his eyes with his hand.

"People are talking. They're saying Hortense was murdered. They're saying she was murdered for her client book because she was blackmailing men who visited her house."

"And were you a client, Monsieur?"

"Not exactly."

"Monsieur," I say "Either you were a client or you were not, what is the answer?"

He shrugs his shoulders and purses his lips before answering. "I used to visit the house occasionally, but I wasn't a client of Hortense. I used to meet Eveline there. She was one of the nieces of Hortense. So you see, Danielle, I might be in the client book but I wasn't being blackmailed and I didn't hurt Hortense. Please believe me."

"We don't even know if she was murdered, Rene," I reply. "There was no evidence of a client book in her house."

"Oh, thank God, thank God, I don't know what I'd do if my Paulette ever found out I visited that house.

You won't tell her will you?"

His eyes are full of tears and his hands are shaking.

"As far as I'm concerned the matter is closed," I reply. "I doubt that I'll need to talk to you on this subject again but rest assured, if I do, I'll be discreet."

"Bless you, Danielle, bless you. It's such a weight off my mind."

With that we both stand and I show him to the door. I watch as he walks away from the office and I note that he seems to have regained his posture. He's standing straight and he's positively striding down the street, but after a few metres he turns and comes back.

"About the Catalan sausage," he says, "If anyone asks you, will you tell them I gave it to you from my van in Ceret? I don't want anyone to know I was here."

"Off course, Monsieur," I agree and I smile at him. "After all we don't want a sausage to get you into trouble, do we?"

He shakes his forefinger at me and smiles then once again he sets off down the street.

CHAPTER 6

I'm so glad when my shift is over and I can leave the office and go home. The day has been full of irritating, petty things and it's been boring and exhausting. The summer heat is relentless and the large glass windows that cover the entire front of the main office make the temperature inside almost unbearable. Even with several fans running the atmosphere is heavy and very draining. The two junior officers, who are working for me at the moment, are going to the café for a beer before they head for home. They invite me to join them and I accept. Patricia won't have dinner ready for at least an hour so it's better if I keep out of her way for a while.

One of the officers, Stephan is his name, raises the subject of Madame Henriette's house. He has managed to contact the next of kin and the young man who is her son will be arriving from Paris at the end of the week. He hasn't seen his mother for several years although they did keep in touch with one another by telephone. We won't know the full story until he gets here but it seems that he's rather well known as a celebrity chef.

"I'm not sure what to do about the house," Stephan says. "Three girls usually work there and they all have keys. Should I tell them to remove their personal belongings and then have the locks changed? Do they have any rights? Can they continue using the house? I just don't know what's right and Raymond, the officer in Ceret, has just gone on annual leave so it's down to us."

"Tell the girls to remove their things and change the locks," I say. "They are prostitutes and their business is illegal, they have no rights. Make sure that they only take their personal belongings and you have a list of everything they remove. If anything doesn't seem right, don't let them remove it. I would like you to take brief statements from the girls as well please."

I'm annoyed that Raymond has gone off on leave because he didn't say anything to me about it, particularly as it was he who stopped this incident from being closed down quickly. Now I'll have to investigate what should have been an open and shut case without being able to pass on most of the work to him.

I am irritated and I quickly finish my beer and say goodbye to my colleagues then leave for home. When I step out of the café the breeze is hot and it feels as if someone is blasting my face with a hairdryer. The car is like an oven and even with all the windows open I've almost reached home before I can breathe comfortably.

When I enter the house I'm given the usual manic welcome from the dog and ignored by the cat. Patricia greets me with an ice-cold glass of apple juice and asks me about my day. I tell her how boring it has been but choose not to mention Rene Charles' visit to me. Instead I give her the news about Madame Henriette's son being a celebrity chef.

"How exciting do you know his name?" she asks.

"Stephan said Albert something but I can't remember. To tell you the truth I was only half listening."

"Not Michel Albert?" she asks excitedly. "He's only the top chef in Paris and he has his own television show."

Patricia is going on and on about Michel Albert and I'm tired. I say rather tetchily, "For goodness sake, Patricia, he's just a cook not a movie star." As soon as the words are out of my mouth I'm sorry for what I've said.

She looks slightly crestfallen and replies, "I'm a just a cook, Danielle, but he is like a movie star."

"You are not just a cook," I reply trying to make amends for my faux pas "You're a marvellous cook and you have a successful business."

I can see I've hurt her but I find it difficult to apologise so instead, after a few moments of awkward silence, I change the subject.

"How was your day?" I question.

Patricia sighs then says, "Do you remember Frederick who I used to work with? He was quite short and going bald and he always wore thick glasses. Frederick was a mortician and his wife Anna worked in the supermarket."

I do remember Frederick. He was very kind and he had a dark sense of humour that I appreciated.

"Well he telephoned me today," she continues. "He's inherited his father's small vineyard and this is his first year as a 'vigneron'. He's looking for help with the 'vendange' as he doesn't have enough pickers. The Syrah grapes will be ready in about two weeks. Can you spare any time?"

I've been grape picking only twice before and it's back breaking work but there's usually a great atmosphere in the fields and Patricia is obviously keen to help out.

"Is this a paying job," I joke.

"Frederick says he has no money to pay us, or indeed any of the pickers, that's why he needs help. However, he's promised to recompense us later in the year with bottles of wine."

"Sounds good to me," I reply. "Let him know I'm prepared to work the Friday and Saturday. That will give me the Sunday to recover before I'm back in the office. Oh, and tell him we're expecting the best of the wine for our labour and a decent meal at the end of each day, and make sure he knows I'm not sleeping in a barn."

"Don't be too hasty in refusing the barn because, from what he's said about the state of the house, the barn might be the best place to sleep."

"Great, I'll pack a tent just in case," I reply and I'm beginning to wonder if I've perhaps made a terrible mistake. I vaguely remember being given advice about never volunteering.

CHAPTER 7

Patricia and I carry our food to the table which is permanently placed in the garden during summer. I've erected a structure over it to give shade and a vine that Patricia planted last year is beginning to entwine itself upwards and over the top. Its leaves throw shadows onto the heavy wooden planks below. It's an idyllic setting, warm but airy, calm and quiet, with the only sounds being the occasional buzz of an insect or the rustle of a bird or rabbit moving about in the undergrowth.

This is my favourite part of the day, sitting here with Patricia and sharing the delicious food she's prepared. We love each other more than sisters and our love is pure and uncomplicated. I marvel at how our lives have changed since we first bought this house together. I look at the food in front of me. It's rich and varied just like our lives have become. With great pleasure I dip a ladle into the Catalan cassoullet Patricia has slow cooked. The pot is full of succulent pieces of pork, chicken, sausage and large, flat, white beans. Then I tear off great chunks of rustic bread to mop up the thick sauce. After eating my fill of the stew, I can almost taste the delicious fruit pie that is to be our dessert as its warm sugary aroma reaches my nostrils and makes me salivate even before one bite passes my lips. Patricia and I laugh and talk and share and I appreciate every wonderful moment I spend with her.

Red Light in the Pyrenees

When we can't eat another bite Patricia clears our plates and I fetch Madame Henriette's diary from the house, then I sit back down at the table to peruse it. I feel I must pass it on to her son, but I want to study it first in case there's sensitive information held within that I should know about. It's not long before I realise that the diary doesn't contain any information about her clients. At least it doesn't contain any names, but events in her life are well recorded. It also has details of bank deposits and bonds and, if I'm reading it correctly, it shows me that Madame Henriette was rather well off financially. After two hours I'm still reading and it has become quite dark. Patricia has cleared everything from the table except for the jug of wine and my glass. She and Ollee have retreated to the house to avoid being bitten by mosquitoes. I decide to make a move, but as I try to lift the jug and my glass, the diary drops from my hand. When I reach down to retrieve it I notice that a thin piece of printed white paper has slipped out from between its pages. I study the paper and realise it's a lottery ticket. Madame Henriette will no longer have a use for this I think and I slip it into my pocket.

After I go inside I feel too hot and wide awake to sleep so I say goodnight to Patricia and she climbs the stairs to her bedroom while I remain in the sitting room. I switch on the television to catch the late night news and near the end of the programme there's an item regarding the unclaimed prize from last week's lottery draw. It's announced that only four out of the five prize winners have come forward. I take the crumpled ticket of Madame Henriette out of my pocket and stare at the numbers and then at the screen. I hold my breath then I stare again, both the ticket and screen have the identical numbers. I feel a jag of excitement and I check them again and again. They're definitely the same. I'm holding the winning ticket. I'm numb with shock, I actually see stars and I think I may faint because the ticket in my shaking hand is worth 200,000 euros. With Madame Henriette dead I can claim the money and no one would be any the wiser. I look at the ticket once more. It's a lucky dip so there are no special numbers, anyone could have bought it.

I feel very emotional and I think I might cry because this money is a fortune and it will secure the future for me and Patricia. I must think carefully about how to get the money and remain anonymous because my life would be hell if anyone found out about it. There would be begging letters from neighbours, distant relatives would crawl out of the woodwork and many people would be jealous of me. I decide there and then that I won't even tell Patricia about the lottery win. If I do tell her anything, I'll lie about the source of the money. I carefully place the ticket in the centre of my wallet and clutch it to my heart. My mind is racing with ideas of how best to invest the money and I change my mind about a hundred times. When I look at my watch it is two-thirty and I'm still wide awake. How can I even think about sleeping on a night like this?

I must eventually have nodded off however, because I'm woken by Ollee's loud snoring. He's climbed upon my lap and his head is resting on my shoulder, his wet nose is pressed against my neck and his tongue is dripping drool down my shirt collar. I gently lift the sleeping dog off me and onto the floor, he stands stiffly and stretches until his tail shakes then he flops back down, gives a loud sigh, then is immediately back in dreamland. I check the ticket in my wallet once again just in case I imagined it all. The numbers are unchanged it wasn't a dream, but I still can't quite believe my good fortune and I feel a stab of fear and apprehension about claiming the money.

CHAPTER 8

I arrive at work early even though I've had hardly any sleep because I wanted to leave home before Patricia had a chance to engage me in conversation. We did exchange a brief 'see you later' as she came down the stairs and I was going out of the door. The ticket is still in my wallet and it's burning a hole in my pocket. I'm anxious to get the claim procedure underway but as soon as I arrive at the office I find myself answering a couple of calls. The first is from an employee of the swimming club who asks if I'll attend the club immediately because they're having a problem with some of the members. The second is from my friend Marjorie.

I arrange for Marjorie to meet me in the café for a 'plat du jour' at one o' clock because, I think, if ever there was a day for mixing business with pleasure this is it. Then I make my way to the municipal swimming pool. The facility is situated at one end of our small town and has recently had a complete makeover with no expense spared. The pool is outdoors and it's very popular with both the local population and tourists alike. Today is the height of summer and the busiest time for tourists so I'm surprised to see that nobody is in the water. In fact the pool looks deserted apart from three colourful floats and a discarded towel.

As I make my way round to the office I can hear raised voices coming from inside. When I open the door I'm completely unprepared for the sight that greets me. The pool attendant, who is a skinny young man in his twenties, is standing between two middle-aged ladies who are shouting at each other. Each of the ladies is seated facing the other and they are hurling abuse like daggers as the young man tries to calm them down. He is holding his hands out in front of him in a placatory fashion, but from the bruising that is rapidly forming around his eye, it looks as if he's already come off rather badly at their hands.

"Thank God you're here, Officer," he says almost crying with relief. "This kicked off in the water and I had to close the pool for everyone's safety. My bosses will freak when they find out, but I was here on my own and I didn't know what else to do. I've already been injured in the fight between this pair and I couldn't risk anyone else being hurt."

The women have stopped shouting but they're still sniping at each other.

"Will you both please be quiet," I say. They are still bitching. "Shut up now or I'll arrest you." That seems to work and finally there is silence. "Which one of you is going to tell me what this is all about?" They both start speaking at once. "Shut up," I shout and once more there is silence. I point to one of the women whose wet hair is dripping onto her face causing her mascara to run in rivulets down her plump cheeks. "You begin, Madame," I say. "And you stay quiet," I order as I point to the other.

"It is all her fault," she begins pointing to the other woman who has now started to cry. "She was in charge of buying the ticket last week. We all gave her the money."

"I did buy the ticket," the other one wails "I showed it to you."

"The ticket that you showed me did not have our numbers. I think you exchanged your own ticket for the one with our winning numbers on it."

"Oh, for goodness sake! It was because I didn't have my glasses with me that I made a mistake when I filled in the form. It was a mistake, a genuine accident, I purchased no other ticket and I did not steal your money."

I interrupt, "Are we speaking about the lottery?" I ask.

"Yes," they answer in unison.

It's all beginning to make sense now.

The pool attendant explains, "They both began shouting at each other in the pool then they climbed out of the water and it became physical, hair pulling, scratching and throwing punches. I tried to intervene. Then this one," he says pointing to the lady who is now sobbing loudly, "Throws a punch and catches me on the eye. I slide on the wet surface and bang my shoulder." He shows me another bruise. "That's when I decided to close the pool and call you."

I'm not sure who, if anyone, I should charge so I suggest that each lady in turn goes and gets changed then returns to the office. When everyone has calmed down a bit I ask, "How long have you had this arrangement for buying the lottery tickets?"

"Two years," they reply in unison.

"And have you ever won a prize before?"

"We've won small prizes several times," one of them answers.

"And has there ever been an incident before when there's been a mistake with your numbers?"

They look sheepishly at one another. "There was one time when Laura bought a lucky dip instead of using our numbers," one of them replies.

"That was one of the times when we won," the other cuts in.

"So mistakes do happen," I reason.

They both nod and now they're both crying.

"Do you want to press charges for assault?" I ask the pool attendant. "You're perfectly within your rights because you've been injured."

"If you would please just sign my accident report Officer, I'll be happy to forget about it. I need something to show my boss to explain why I closed the pool. I really just want to lock up and go home."

The sobbing women look relieved and, with my permission, they gather up their belongings and leave the office. I stay and help the young man close up the place then I drive him home. It just goes to show you how money can change people and sometimes for the worse. But I get such a thrill whenever I think about my lottery ticket and how it could change my life for the better.

CHAPTER 9

When I arrive at the café for my lunch with Marjorie the place is jumping and every table is full, mostly with tourists. They all seem to be wearing the tourist uniform of shorts and t-shirts and the level of noise is almost unbearable. It only takes me a moment to spot Marjorie she is, as usual, impeccably dressed and therefore stands out from the rabble. Today she's wearing a figure hugging, grey coloured, straight skirt with a tailored blouse that accentuates her feminine curves. She's wearing her hair shoulder length at the moment and it's coloured a rich brown. Her makeup is light and perfect. On the seat beside her she has casually discarded her bag and her jacket and on the table in front of her is a 'demi pichet de rouge'. I notice she's already poured herself a glass of the deep red wine and that's unusual for Marjorie. French women of a good class rarely drink alcohol in the middle of the day and they are almost never seen drinking alone in public. For the wife of the Mayor it could be considered most inappropriate.

When I arrive at her table she stands and shakes my hand. Had I not been in uniform she would have kissed me on both cheeks. The people around us stare at me for a moment or two. The uniform has that effect on folk. They're hoping that if the police are around something exciting is going to happen. However everyone settles down when I pick up the menu and they realise, that like them, I am simply here to dine.

"Thank you for coming, Danielle," Marjorie says. "I think you know why I wanted this meeting."

"Based on what you said on the phone, I assume it's about the recent death in Ceret," I reply.

"That's correct but I would prefer not to discuss it here. Let us eat and then perhaps we can take a walk and talk if it's okay with you."

"For you anything my friend," I reply and I sincerely mean what I say. Marjorie's friendship means the world to Patricia and me.

We both opt for a plate of 'charcuterie' and 'crudités' as it's too warm for hot food. Service is rather slow but nobody seems to mind as most of the people here are on holiday. There are only two waiters working a large number of tables and they are taking time to make small talk with the tourists, because the British in particular are known to be good tippers. One of the local dogs is also working the tables. She walks about sniffing the air and when she smells something she likes she sidles up to the diners, stares at them and wags her tail. She has a sweet face and a gentle manner and her actions rarely fail to win her a tasty morsel or two.

I pour myself a glass of wine and Marjorie finishes the 'pichet'. She is obviously very nervous and after we have our coffees she insists on paying the bill.

"I invited you," she says. "Please allow me the pleasure of treating you."

When the bill is paid we leave the restaurant and start to walk in the direction of the river. We cross over at the bridge and walk past the petanque players then take a seat on a bench at a quiet part of the riverbank. I look around me to ensure there's no one about who could overhear us. Marjorie is biting her bottom lip nervously and her hands are tightly clasped in her lap.

"When I visited the house of Madame Henriette on the morning her body was discovered I found no trace of a client book," I begin. "I removed her diary and I've been through it. It makes no mention of any clients."

Marjorie inhales deeply and her eyes fill with tears. She reaches into her handbag, removes a handkerchief, and blows her nose loudly.

"Thank you Danielle. I'm so relieved," she says. "My husband is such a good man, but like most men, he can be weak and stupid. He used to tell me he was playing cards once a month but I knew he was lying to me. I knew he was visiting that house."

"Weren't you angry with him? Didn't you feel that he was betraying you?" I ask unable to stop myself.

"My husband is kind and gentle and he provides well for me and the children. He is a decent, honest man and everyone respects him. There aren't many men who'd give me the sort of life I enjoy. I'd be naïve to get upset about one misdemeanour, one little weakness. It doesn't mean he loves me any less, quite the reverse in fact. He visits this girl who he doesn't love. She means nothing to him. It's simply a business transaction. It's not as if he's taken a mistress who'd take his money and flaunt her relationship in my face."

It never ceases to amaze me that so many French

women will accept the bad behaviour of their husbands, providing it doesn't cause them to lose face and providing it doesn't affect their lifestyle.

"I can tell you, Danielle, on the day Madame Henriette met her death, my husband was at home looking after our son who had taken ill at school. Audrey, my cleaner, can confirm this. I was at the hairdresser because in the evening we were entertaining members of the Charity Committee in our home. He was nowhere near the house of Madame Henriette that day."

"Thank you, Marjorie," I reply "But it's not necessary for you to tell me this. I still believe Madame Henriette's death was an unfortunate accident and I'm hopeful I'll soon be able to close the door on this whole affair. As there's no client book, and therefore no mention of anyone, your husband's whereabouts are of no interest to me or anyone else. As far as I'm concerned he's had no connection whatsoever with that house or anyone in it."

"Bless you, Danielle," she says gripping my hand and pressing it to her lips. "I'll never forget your kindness."

I feel slightly embarrassed by this show of affection and gratitude so I stand and tell her that I must now get back to work. We walk together in silence until we reach the bridge then we go our separate ways. I am conscious that the day is rapidly coming to an end and I have yet to discover how to claim my lottery prize.

CHAPTER 10

When I arrive back at the office I'm informed that my superior in Perpignan has called and he wants me to get in touch as soon as possible. I'm curious to know what he wants because recently Detective Gerard has pretty much let me run my own show. I pour myself a coffee and call his number and he answers on the third ring.

"Thank you for getting back to me so quickly, Danielle," he says. "This is rather a delicate matter so I'll get straight to the point. It's regarding Officer Dupree."

Officer Dupree, I think, that's Raymond, his surname is Dupree.

"I'm afraid he's on annual leave, Sir," I reply.

"Yes, Danielle, he is on leave at my suggestion. He telephoned me after the body of Madame Henriette was discovered. I know he should have contacted you first but it was a private matter of great delicacy and he felt he couldn't discuss it with a woman, so I'll apologise on his behalf."

I'm absolutely livid, how dare Raymond go over my head. I'm his superior first and a woman second as far as the law is concerned.

"Can you enlighten me now?" I ask.

"But of course, Danielle. It seems that Officer Dupree was a client of Madame Henriette. He used to visit a girl named Veronique once a week."

I am completely shocked. Raymond is a single, young man and he's not bad looking. Why ever would he visit a prostitute and take such a risk in his position? I just cannot understand it.

"I see," is all I can reply.

"Anyway, he seems to think that Madame Henriette had a client book and it's missing. He's searched the house from top to bottom but there's no sign of it. He told me you removed a diary but not a client book. Is that correct?"

"Yes, that is true. I found no client book," I reply. "What makes Officer Dupree so sure that one exists?"

"The whore he visited used to boast that Madame and her girls would retire one day. She said the names of the rich men noted in the book would be a licence to print money. She told Officer Dupree that if he kept his mouth shut his name would be removed from the book. He thinks Madame Henriette's death might be more than an accident. He thinks she may have been murdered for the book."

"So let me understand." I say. "Officer Dupree regularly visited a whorehouse. He believed the ramblings of a prostitute. If such a book exists, and I don't believe it does, surely he'd be the prime suspect if it was stolen. This whole business makes no sense to me. Doctor Poullet and I both immediately thought the death looked like an unfortunate accident. It was Officer Dupree who pushed for further investigation."

"Perhaps he has something to hide. Perhaps he has a guilty conscience. All we can do at this stage is keep him off duty and fully investigate. The book might not exist but Dupree believes it does. So if there's even the whisper of a chance that he was involved in Madame Henriette's death we can't ignore it."

"I fully agree with you, Sir," I reply, "I'll speak to Officer Dupree myself. I'll be very discreet. None of my team will know of his involvement and I'll try to close this case down as soon as possible. Between you and me, I don't believe he has it in him to commit murder. He's very meek and mild and I think that's the reason for him visiting the house in the first place. He's probably too shy to ask girls out."

"I hope to God you're right, Danielle because if you're wrong the consequences don't bear thinking about."

When I finish the call I think about what I've been told and I'm very concerned. Raymond may know the identity of other visitors to the house and I hope he doesn't shoot his mouth off and name names. I must consider this information very carefully and I must tread very gently because Raymond might be a loose cannon.

CHAPTER 11

I decide to bite the bullet and get Raymond's phone number from the system and I call him. I tell Raymond that I've spoken to Detective Gerard and we both feel it would be better for me to speak to him and get his statement as soon as possible. He's very upset and, quite understandably, he doesn't want to discuss the matter either here or at the office in Ceret where there's the risk of his colleagues overhearing. We finally agree that I'll visit his house at six-thirty and I assure him I'll be very discreet. Firstly, however, I intend to go and collect the keys for Madame Henriette's house from Raymond's office as it is no longer appropriate for him to have access. Before I leave I instruct my colleagues to take in-depth statements from Madame Henriette's employees with particular emphasis on any client book or records.

After I pick up the keys from Raymond's desk drawer, I check the house and make sure that everything is properly closed up. I have half an hour to kill before my meeting so I decide to use the time to try and discover how to claim on the winning lottery ticket. Then I walk briskly round the corner to the local newsagent as this seems to be the best place to start.

"Bonjour, Monsieur," I say to the newsagent, "I would like to buy a lottery ticket."

There are a couple of men in the shop and I see that they've each bought a strip of several tickets.

They're showing them to each other and discussing the numbers.

"Just one ticket, Officer?" the newsagent asks and he and the other men exchange glances and laugh. They seem to find it hilarious that I would try to win with just one ticket.

"Is there a problem, Monsieur?" I ask. They are now guffawing and repeating the words 'one ticket.' I'm beginning to get irritated by their childish behaviour and I don't like them making jokes at my expense.

"No, no, of course not," he says. "After all you just need one lucky ticket to win. Although it is said, that with only one ticket, you stand more chance of being murdered than having the winning numbers."

"Look at Madame Henriette," one of the men begins. "She always bought one ticket in this very shop every Monday and now she is dead, perhaps murdered, so maybe the statistics are correct."

I stare at the men and they stare back at me. They now seem very serious and I'm beginning to feel quite uncomfortable when suddenly the three of them explode into laughter once again.

"I don't think you're funny," I continue. "Death is no laughing matter."

This makes them laugh all the more.

"Should I survive the draw and be blessed with the winning numbers how do I claim my large prize?" I ask.

"That's the easy part," one of the men answers. "You simply telephone the claim line number and the claim manager arranges for you to complete a form. Then, when everything is checked and they are sure the ticket is genuine, they give you the money."

"Where do you get this claim line number?" I ask.

"You can get it online, but as you're so sure of winning with your one ticket, I'll write the phone number down for you," the newsagent offers. "Just remember, when you're a millionaire, that I sold you the winning ticket."

I hand over my money and I take the ticket and telephone number. I'm delighted because, not only do I know how to make a claim on my ticket, I also know when and where the ticket was bought. I can hear the men laughing at me as I leave the shop, but I don't care because I'm the one with a winning ticket and the means to collect the money

I arrive at Raymond's home at exactly six-thirty and press the button of the interphone. Nobody answers, but the buzzer sounds to release the front door and I take the lift to the second floor apartment. Madame Dupree, Raymond's mother, is at the open front door and Raymond is standing behind her with an exasperated look on his face.

"Bonsoir, Madame," I say. "My name is Danielle. I am a colleague of Raymond's."

Raymond's mother is a small, plump woman with a plain face and sandy coloured hair. She's wearing a floral patterned apron and she's holding a dish towel in her hand. Madame Dupree steps aside to let me enter, offers coffee which I refuse, then she scuttles off to the kitchen leaving Raymond and me in the hallway.

"I'm sorry about my mother," he says. "She likes to know everything that's going on," he explains. "Please come into the front room."

He ushers me through a door into a large room and offers me a seat on the sofa. The room is full of large, old-fashioned pieces of furniture and there are ornaments displayed on every surface. Raymond is sweating with nerves and he constantly wipes his face with a cotton handkerchief.

"I'm finding this very difficult," he says. "I didn't come to you directly because I'm very embarrassed by my behaviour. If you were a married lady it wouldn't be so bad but because you're single I feel ashamed. I hope you're not angry because I spoke directly to Detective Gerard, I meant no disrespect, quite the opposite in fact."

"I understand your position, Raymond," I reply. "There are no hard feelings," I lie. "Let's just get this over with, shall we?"

I try to keep the meeting as formal as possible and after twenty minutes my notes are complete. I caution Raymond and advise him that until the investigation is complete he'll be on extended leave. I also warn him that if this case does prove to be murder then he'll be considered a suspect. He's completely shocked and stunned by this.

"But how can I possibly be suspected?" he asks. "I'm the one who came forward with the evidence."

"That was perhaps rather naïve of you," I reply.

"Of course you'll be a suspect because you have much to gain by her death. You admitted you were in a position to be blackmailed by Madame Henriette, did you not?"

"Oh my God, what have I done? How can I possibly explain to my mother why I'm not going in to work? If this goes on for any length of time people will find out I visited that house. People will know. They'll think I'm some kind of a pervert. My life will be ruined and my mother will be shamed."

I say nothing but I'm secretly pleased by his distress because I'm still angry he went over my head.

"Is there anything you can do to help me?" he pleads.

"I'm so sorry, Raymond, but it's out of my hands now. If you'd come directly to me we could have ended this matter and closed the case because Doctor Poullet was satisfied the death was accidental. Unfortunately, now that Gerard is involved, I must follow procedure and investigate every aspect of Madame Henriette and her business. So you see I cannot help you."

He nods slowly and his face is a picture of misery. Serves him right I think to myself. He's a disgrace to his mother and a disgrace to his uniform and he deserves all he gets.

CHAPTER 12

As I drive home the heat becomes very oppressive and I can feel the pressure in the atmosphere that usually heralds a storm. By the time I reach the house the sky is beginning to blacken. I call to Patricia as I enter the door to advise her to rescue the washing from the line before the heavens open. She thanks me and asks me to help by retrieving the cushions from the chairs outside. We are just in time as some huge drops of rain are beginning to fall.

When we are seated, enjoying our meal, Patricia asks me about my day. I talk about my lunch with Marjorie and she's pleased that I have reassured our friend. I don't mention my meeting with Raymond Dupree. I ask her what she's been up to and she tells me that she took some fruit pies to the church hall this afternoon for the Retirement Club's meeting.

"I spent some time speaking to Monsieur Gainsboro," she says. "He's a lovely man. He lives in a house near the centre of the village."

"Is that the gentleman whose son owns the electrical shop in town?" I ask.

"Yes, that's right. The whole family are really nice. Monsieur Gainsboro is planning to move in with his son because he's finding his house too much to manage on his own. He's selling his house to a couple from England."

"He does live rather far from the shops," I say.

"So it'll be much better for him to be in town."

Patricia seems to be thinking about something. She has stopped eating and her chin is resting on her hand.

"Are you free tomorrow morning?" she begins. "There's something I want you to see."

"This sounds serious," I reply. "Should I be worried?" I pull a mock frightened face.

"You can be so silly sometimes," she answers laughing. "I want you to look at the small orchard that Monsieur Gainsboro owns. He's not selling it as part of the house sale. I think it would be perfect for me. I know we don't have much cash to spare, and he probably wants a lot of money for it, but I'd still like to look at it if you don't mind."

I look at her sweet face, her blue eyes are sparkling and she is full of expectation. I love her so much and I would do anything within my power to make her happy.

"Of course we'll look at it," I reply, "I'll take a couple of hours off tomorrow morning. It won't be a problem because I worked late this evening so I'm owed the time."

I feel so excited about the orchard because I know that I can afford to buy it for her, whatever the price. All I have to do is claim on my lottery ticket and I can give her anything she wants. Once again, when I go to bed, I lie awake for hours because the excitement has got the better of me. However, when I do wake in the morning, after only a couple of hours sleep, I feel surprisingly refreshed.

After a rushed breakfast we meet Monsieur Gainsboro at the orchard at nine o'clock and I'm pleased that the ground has dried after last night's rain. Monsieur Gainsboro is a lovely man. He greets us both formally with a handshake then places his hands on either side of Patricia's face and plants kisses on her cheeks. He shows us into the orchard through a rather rickety gate and we are faced with a beautiful field of trees and flowering grass.

"The flowering grasses are good for the trees because they attract the insects for pollination," he explains. "It's quite a small orchard as you can see but I've cared for it well and the trees produce a lot of fruit. There are four apple trees, four cherry trees, six of apricot and the two trees at the back are hazelnut."

"It's amazing, wonderful, I love it," Patricia says. "I'd love to buy it Monsieur Gainsboro but as you know we have only recently bought our house so there isn't much money to spare."

"How much is the sale price?" I cut in.

"I'm looking for fifteen thousand euros," he replies. "I think it's a fair price, don't you agree?"

Patricia bites her lip and says nothing, I can see she's disappointed because it's a large amount of money and it would normally be completely out of her reach.

"I think it's a very fair price, Monsieur," I reply. "We will, of course, need time to consider it."

"Of course," he replies. "There's no rush, there aren't many people queuing up to buy orchards during these difficult financial times. Take all the time you need and, if anyone else shows an interest, I'll telephone you before I make any decision."

I thank Monsieur Gainsboro and lead Patricia back to the car.

"I have to go to work now, so I'll take you back home then I'll set off," I say.

"It is a beautiful orchard isn't it?" she asks. "I'm so glad we saw it even if we can't afford it because it gives me something to aspire to."

She's resigned herself to the fact that it's out of her reach but it might not be out of mine. I'll feel more comfortable about it when I call the lottery claim line later today.

When I get to the office my colleagues have both made appointments in the afternoon to interview Madame Henriette's former employees. I'm informed that one of them is to speak to Eva, the maid, at her home and the other is to interview Phoebe, one of Madame's 'nieces', at the office. Eveline, one of the other prostitutes, has arranged her interview for tomorrow morning. As yet, we have been unable to contact the third girl, Veronique. I'm concerned that we're having difficulty tracing her as she was the girl visited by Raymond Dupree. She was also the one who talked about the client book.

When my colleagues leave the office for lunch I lock the door and take the lottery ticket from my wallet. My hands are shaking so much that I can hardly read the numbers on it. I place it on the desk in front of me along with the claim line telephone number then I pour myself a coffee and try to calm down. It takes me three attempts before I can successfully dial the number as I'm so nervous. The phone is answered almost immediately by a young woman and I tell her that I think I have the fifth winning ticket from last week's draw. She asks me to verify the numbers on my ticket, which I do. Then she takes my name and contact telephone number and asks me to hold the line.

"Bonjour, Danielle. May I call you Danielle?" an enthusiastic male voice booms down the phone. "I believe congratulations are in order. My name is Alain and I'm your claim manager."

"B-b bonjour, Alain," I stutter, "Yes, you may call me Danielle."

"We were wondering when, or if in fact, you would come forward. Most people who win the jackpot contact us right away."

"I didn't realise I'd won because I forgot to check my ticket," I reply lamely. "It was only when there was an announcement on the television, that one winner was still outstanding, I remembered to look at it."

"Well congratulations from all of us at Lottery HQ. Now let me explain to you what happens next. Firstly, someone from our company must verify that you are indeed the holder of the winning ticket. Once this is established we'll ask you to complete a form giving your personal details. We'll also ask how you came by the winning ticket. For example, was it gifted to you, or did you buy it yourself? If you did buy it yourself, we'll want to know details such as when and where you purchased it, etcetera. Are we clear so far?"

"Yes, thank you," I reply. "How and when will this take place?" I ask.

"You live near Perpignan," he states. "I can be with you tomorrow morning."

"I don't want anyone to know that I've won," I say.

"That's not a problem," he replies. "However, we do recommend if you have a husband or partner who lives with you, that you tell them. Because it's very difficult to keep a secret of this magnitude from a close loved one."

I immediately picture Patricia's sweet face and I must admit that the thought of telling her does give me a thrill.

"I would ask you to keep your ticket in a very safe place. You might also want to consider how you would like the money to be paid to you. As you wish to remain anonymous a presentation at a lottery party with the press around is out of the question. So your prize cannot be handed over by a film star or a celebrity, but we can discuss your options when we meet."

Alain offers to come to my house but I'd prefer if we didn't meet there so he gives me an address of a hotel in Perpignan. He tells me to ask for a 'Monsieur Blanc' at the reception desk. We are to meet at 10 o'clock and he reminds me to bring my winning ticket together with photo ID. Alain gives me his mobile number and his direct number at the office in case there is any change of plan, or if I have any further questions. Then with more words of congratulations, he is gone.

I sit and sip my now cold coffee and I feel dazed. I can't believe this is happening to me and by this time tomorrow I'll be 200,000 euros richer.

CHAPTER 13

After the excitement of my phone call the afternoon passes slowly with no one calling at the office and not a single telephone enquiry either. My colleagues arrive back in time for us to close up for the day and, from the meagre statements they've taken from the girls they interviewed, I think most of their time has been spent in a café or a bar.

According to the girls, neither of them saw or heard anything and they have no knowledge of a client book. They didn't know the true names of any of the men who visited the house and they would not be able to recognise any of them if they saw them again. When pressed, Eveline said she always kept her eyes shut during sex, so of course she could not recognise anything about the men. Talking to them was a total waste of time but that's alright because, once we've spoken to the other two girls, we can close the book on this case as there will be nothing else to investigate. I just need to locate Veronique and I'll be home and dry.

As I drive home I keep getting a surge of excitement when I think about the money I'm going to receive but I'll not say anything to Patricia until it's in the bank. In my mind I go over and over the things I want to do with it but, most importantly, I want to buy Patricia the orchard as a surprise. Fifteen thousand euros seems like such a small sum now, and owning that piece of land will give her business and her spirits such a boost. I rehearse lots of different ways of telling her about the orchard and all of them end with her squealing with delight and being overcome with emotion. When I arrive home and enter the garden Ollee starts running round and round like a maniac.

"He's been like that all day," Patricia says. "He's just so happy and excitable at the moment. It must be the changing season, maybe he's sensing that the temperature will soon become more bearable and it's giving him more energy."

"And how are you?" I ask. "Are you happy and excitable at the moment? I know I am" I say, then I leap about and I pretend to pant, Ollee starts to bark and I bark back at him. Patricia is laughing at us.

"You are both absolutely mad," she says. "I am living with crazy people. Did your day go well?" she asks. "You seem very upbeat."

"Yes, thank you" I reply, "I've had a very productive day."

"I finished my painting this morning," she says. "I just have to deliver it to the gallery in Perpignan and I can collect my cheque. They've already sold it and I'm to be paid four hundred euros. It's quite large so if there's a day that you can take me in the car I'd be very grateful."

"How about tomorrow? I've to run an errand in Perpignan in the morning so I can drop you at the gallery then pick you up and bring you home at lunchtime."

"That would be fantastic," she says. "I have been thinking a lot recently because of Monsieur

Gainsboro's orchard coming up for sale. I'd like to take ten per cent of everything I earn and save it in a separate account in the bank. Then in the future, if a big opportunity comes along, I'll have a deposit to put down and the bank might consider me for a loan. Of course I'll only do this if you agree," she adds.

She looks at me expectantly and I'm amazed at her determination.

"I love you," I say and I feel myself filling up with emotion. "Everything you do and say makes me happy. My life is perfect with you."

She walks up behind me and puts her arms round my waist and rests her head on my back.

"I love you too," she says. "But enough of this mushiness it's time to eat and it's your turn to do the washing up tonight. So don't think you can sweet talk me into doing it because it just won't work."

After dinner we go up to my bedroom and climb into bed. We talk for hours discussing everything from mending the chicken house to Marjorie's errant husband. It is lucky that I thought to set the alarm clock because it's well after one o'clock when we turn out the light to go to sleep. I can't risk sleeping late because tomorrow is a very important day.

CHAPTER 14

It's eight thirty in the morning and I'm pacing the floor with nerves. Patricia's painting is carefully stowed in the car and my uniform is also there so that I can change into it after my meeting. Patricia isn't ready to leave yet and, although I have plenty of time, I'm agitated because I'm rather terrified of what lies ahead this morning but exhilarated at the same time.

"Will you get a move on," I finally shout as the tension gets the better of me. "The traffic might be bad at Le Boulou and I can't be late for my appointment."

"Okay, okay I'm nearly ready," she replies. "I'm just making sure that I have everything I need. By the way, did I tell you that you're wonderful?"

She rushes through the door with her package, her bag and her keys in her hands and throws me a winning smile. "Ready," she announces.

"At last," I reply. "You could walk to Perpignan in the time it takes you to get ready."

Ollee has resigned himself to the fact that he's going to be left at home and he follows me into the garden and settles himself on an old blanket which is under the table. It's his favourite place in the garden because it is cool and comfortable and he has a view of the front gate so he can see who comes and goes.

After two attempts, because Patricia forgets something else and has to run back into the house, we are finally on our way. She's chattering away to me but

I'm too nervous to add much to the conversation and my hands are slippery with sweat as I grip the steering wheel.

"Are you okay, Danielle?" she asks. "You're very quiet this morning. Is something wrong?"

"I'm sorry, Patricia," I reply. "I have a very important meeting this morning and I can think of nothing else. Please forgive me."

"Here I am talking rubbish while you're trying to concentrate on your work. I'm sorry."

I feel a bit guilty but everything I've said is true. The rest of the journey passes in silence until we reach the gallery. I help Patricia carry her painting inside, then she hugs me and wishes me all the best for my meeting. If only she knew the truth, I think. We arrange that I'll pick her up from here at one o'clock and I'll telephone her mobile if my meeting overruns, then I get back into the car and head for the Hotel Regina.

I manage to park close to the hotel and enter the majestic front door with much trepidation then I ask for Monsieur Blanc at the reception desk. The concierge makes a brief phone call.

"He'll be with you shortly, Madame," he informs me. "Please take a seat over there." He indicates towards a sofa facing the front desk.

I don't have to wait long as almost as soon as I sit down Alain appears and introduces himself to me. He shakes my hand vigorously.

"Please follow me," he says and I find myself being led into a small meeting room. "Would you like some coffee?" he asks and I nod an acceptance. My mouth is too dry to speak. "Please don't be nervous these formalities will only take a few minutes then we can discuss what you want to do with your money."

I immediately visualise Monsieur Gainsboro's orchard, but I'm sure that Alain is speaking about more practical considerations. He asks for my ticket and my photo ID and I hand him both items. He attaches a device to his computer which is already set up on the table in front of us. It seems to be some sort of bar code reader because he passes the bar code on my ticket in front of it and something immediately flashes up on the computer screen. I'm gripping my knees in terror and my knuckles are white.

"Well, Danielle," he says smiling. "It is an original ticket, but of course you already knew that, and I can confirm it's the missing winning ticket, so congratulations."

I exhale my bated breath and release the grip on my knees.

"Now for the boring bit," he continues and he produces a form from his briefcase.

It takes about fifteen minutes to complete the form, which is mostly asking my personal details and details about where and when I bought the ticket, which of course, I know. Once the form is complete he attaches a portable printer to the computer and prints me off a receipt for my ticket, then he hands back my photo ID.

"Now all that remains is for me to arrange payment of your winnings," he says.

I'm given three options, wire transfer to my cheque account or savings account, or it can be paid into a new bank account. As Patricia and I have a joint account I opt for the latter. I'm advised that the lottery company won't release the money for forty-eight hours, to give them time to complete final checks on the information I've given them.

"I'm at your disposal for the remainder of the day," Alain says. "My company has an arrangement with the bank, Credit Agricole. We could go there now and open your new account, if you wish. I telephoned them this morning and they're standing by just in case."

"They have a branch near my office," I reply, "So that would be handy for me."

I try to stand up and I stagger slightly. Alain puts out his hand to steady me.

"Are you feeling alright?" he asks and he looks at me with concern. "You've become rather pale. Can I get you anything?"

"Just the money," I reply with a smile as I regain my composure.

The next hour passes in a blur. The bank manger is sworn to secrecy and for that reason he completes all the paperwork himself. I'm advised the money will be available for my use within two working days and I'm given all sorts of paperwork and receipts. Alain offers to take me to lunch but I decline explaining that I must meet up with my friend then I have to go to work.

"You mean you're not going to take the rest of the day off?" he asks incredulously. "You must be dedicated. I personally would take the rest of the week off if I ever won the lottery."

Now that everything has been completed, I can't get away from Alain quickly enough. I don't want to be seen with this man any longer. He's too polished and sophisticated and he makes me feel awkward although he's done nothing wrong, on the contrary, he's been very kind to me. Alain gives me the contact details of the financial advisor his company recommends and I shake his hand, then we go our separate ways. It's only when I'm on my own in the street that the enormity of what has just taken place hits me and I practically run for the safety of my parked car. I sit in the car and cry with relief. It's over. I've done it. The money will soon be in my new bank account. The winnings are mine.

I pick up Patricia at the arranged time and she waves her cheque at me triumphantly.

"Let me buy you lunch," she says. "I've been paid and I'm a rich woman."

If only she knew I think to myself, if only she knew.

CHAPTER 15

When I arrive back in the office my colleague is on the phone. His chair is tilted back against the wall and his feet are crossed at the ankles and resting on the wastepaper bin. He has a long suffering look on his face and, when he sees me, he covers the mouthpiece and rolls his eyes.

"She's been talking for ten minutes about dog poo," he informs me nodding at the receiver, "Ten solid minutes without a break.

He hands me a single typewritten sheet of paper.

"My interview with Phoebe the prostitute," he explains. "It's just like with the other girls. She saw and heard nothing and she knows nothing. Still no sign of Veronique," he adds.

I take the paper and drop it into the file with the others without even bothering to read it, then I go into the toilet and change into my uniform. I've just sat down at my desk when my mobile phone starts ringing and when I look at the screen I see it's a call from Raymond Dupree. I'm in two minds whether to answer it or to let the machine take a message, but I reason, I'll have to speak to him at some point and it might as well be now.

"Raymond," I say.

"Help me. Please help me. It's terrible. She's dead. Oh God, she's dead." Raymond is distraught. He is sobbing and practically screaming down the phone.

"Raymond where are you? Who's dead?" I ask.

"Help me, Danielle, please," he begs. "I'm going to be sick. I'm sorry."

I hear him retching. I cover the mouthpiece so that he can't hear me and I call to my colleague. "Hang up the phone now, Paul. I need you. We have an emergency."

He can see by the look on my face that something is seriously wrong. "We're going to need Dr Poullet and the paramedics," is all I can manage to say before Raymond is back on the line.

"She's dead. My poor, poor girl is dead."

"Where are you?"I repeat.

"I am at Veronique's apartment in St Jean," he says and he breaks into wracking sobs. "I tried to save her, but it was too late. She's cold. She's very, very cold."

I manage to get the address from him and I tell him I'm on my way. I keep Raymond talking on the phone while Paul contacts the paramedics and Dr Poullet then we both make for my car. I give Paul the car keys so he can drive while I keep reassuring Raymond. We break every speed limit as we race towards St Jean. My car screeches to a halt outside the apartment block just as the paramedics are arriving. I don't wait for them but instead jump from my car and run inside. The sight that greets me is so shocking I can hardly take it in. Raymond is crouched in the corner of the room cradling his phone and to his left is a sink full of vomit. The room has been completely trashed. There's a naked girl lying on the bed across the room from Raymond. It's obvious she's dead. Every inch of her body is battered and bruised. A bloody hammer lies on the bed beside her.

I go over to Raymond, take the phone from his hand and end the call. He's completely silent now and I can see he's in deep shock. One of the paramedics attends to him as another has a quick look at the body.

"We'll have to take him to the hospital for treatment but there's nothing we can do for that one," the paramedic says, nodding at the body on the bed.

There is a noise from the front door. "Get out of the way you stupid woman. There's nothing for you to see. Let me enter I am a doctor."

The unmistakeable voice of Dr Poullet in his usual good humour I think to myself. He enters the room and looks around and I can see that even he is shocked.

"Can some of you people leave," he demands. "There is no room to move in this tiny studio."

The paramedic who's attending to Raymond helps him to his feet and gently leads him from the room and his colleague leaves with them.

"Bonjour, Danielle," Dr Poullet says recovering his composure. "This is horrible, very, very nasty." He examines the body. "Someone has tortured this poor girl. They have broken her fingers and toes with the hammer and every inch of her body is bruised. Perhaps they were looking for answers that they didn't get."

"She was one of the prostitutes who worked for Madame Henriette," I tell him.

"Ah," he replies, "And the young man, was he

her customer?"

"He's a police officer," I reply. "He's admitted to having a connection with her but I don't think he had anything to do with this. I believe he found her already dead."

"Poor chap, no wonder he's in such a state. There's no doubt here, Danielle, this one is definitely murder."

I'd better contact Detective Gerard, I think to myself, because a police officer is involved. Why couldn't Raymond leave well alone? Why did he have to get involved with this girl? That stupid man and his raging hormones have caused problems for me. Now his interference in this incident is causing it to spiral out of my control.

CHAPTER 16

As Paul stands guard at the front door to keep out the curious, which is no mean feat, Dr Poullet and I find ourselves alone with the corpse.

"Surely someone must have heard something," he says. "This poor girl suffered greatly before she died."

"Was she killed with the hammer?" I ask.

"No, my dear, she was killed with the rope in the cellar," he replies and laughs. I look quizzically at him. "Have you never played the game of 'Cluedo'?" he enquires. "Forgive my humour but sometimes when one is faced with incomprehensible horror the best defence is laughter," he explains. "As it happens, the hammer blows didn't kill her, they were used merely to cause pain she was, in fact, strangled. I assume she was murdered by a man because whoever strangled her did it with their bare hands and not many women are that strong. When someone is fighting for their life the adrenalin rush gives them the strength of a tiger. It's actually much harder to kill someone than it appears on television."

"I better get my camera from the car," I say. "But the room is in such a state I don't know where to start."

"Forget it, Danielle," Doctor Poullet says. "This mess is beyond us. A few photographs and a discussion between ourselves aren't going to be good enough on this occasion. You'll need to call in the big guns from Perpignan and a forensic team and we have to get out of here because we're contaminating the crime scene. Give yourself a break this time, just lock up and walk away. With a bit of luck your boss will let you be the lead on the investigation. Then you'll have all the resources and all of the glory but not too much of the hard slog."

He's right of course. I was so caught up in the incident that I didn't really stop to think. There's no way I can handle this myself. I can't even release the body to the morgue until the forensic team have been in, so I get on the phone right away and call for help.

When I speak to Detective Gerard, he immediately gives me a list of things to do and people to contact and within an hour the investigation takes on a life of its own. He has to attend a conference in Paris so he has no choice but to let me head the investigation. Dr Poullet was correct, all glory and little of the work. I'm delighted. As soon as the forensic people arrive I hand over to them and I head for home. There's nothing more I can do until the morning.

I make a detour so I can drive past the orchard because I need some fresh air before I go home. When I arrive I park beside the gate then enter the orchard. It's larger than I remember and there's actually room to plant more trees, perhaps as many as six more.

Every time I think about the lottery win I get a thrill. Soon all this will be Patricia's, every tree and every blade of grass will belong to her. I take my wallet out of my pocket and search for the piece of paper where I wrote Monsieur Gainsboro's number and when I find it I telephone him.

"Bonsoir, Danielle," he says, "Ca va?"

We exchange pleasantries then I get down to business.

"I wish to buy your orchard, Monsieur," I begin, "I have some money saved and I want to buy it for Patricia. However, there is just one thing I must ask of you, it's to be a surprise, so you can't say anything to her at this stage."

"But of course, of course, I'll say nothing. What a kind sister you are. Patricia will be delighted. She has often purchased fruit from my trees and now they'll belong to her."

I'm sure he knows that Patricia and I aren't sisters, but if it makes him happy to believe we are, I won't correct him. It's much harder for people of his generation to accept that friends can simply want to live together as a family.

"How soon do you want to transact our business?" he enquires.

"As soon as possible," I reply.

"Very well, I'll contact the notaire and we can draw up the 'compromis de vente' as soon as he's available. If you have the money we can conclude the bargain within the next two weeks. That will give Patricia most of the apple crop and all of the hazel nuts."

"That's wonderful Monsieur Gainsboro," I say. "You've made me very happy."

"It's been a long time since a pretty young

woman has said that to me," he replies.

Cheeky old dog I think, I bet he broke a few hearts in his day.

CHAPTER 17

It's Saturday morning and I can't believe it's been only one week since the death of Madame Henriette because so much has happened. I feel very tired and I'm actually looking forward to helping Frederick and Anna with the grape harvest next week, anything to get away from my work and let my brain rest. This morning I'm due to meet with Madame Henriette's son, Michel Albert, to discuss the death of his mother and I'm not looking forward to it. I'm not sure how to handle a celebrity.

When I arrive at the office there's a small group of women outside. Some are holding pictures of the chef and some are clutching autograph books.

"They were here before me," Paul says. "The word is out that Michel Albert is in town and they all want to meet him. I've never seen such a thing, all this fuss over a cook."

"A celebrity chef," I correct. "To them he's a film star."

"C'est ridicule, absolument, ridicule," he says with disgust and I have to admit I agree with him.

"By the time he arrives he won't be able to get through that door," I say. "Perhaps I should call him and arrange to meet him elsewhere."

"I don't think that's a good idea because, at least if he's here we can keep them out of the office, you might get mobbed somewhere else," Paul replies.

"Besides, he is due here in half an hour it's a bit late for a change of plan. I have an idea though, I'll tell the women he's not arriving until the afternoon and they can come back then. I'll say that they must keep the pavement clear or I'll be forced to charge them with loitering and, with a bit of luck, they'll move on."

"But we're not open this afternoon we're closing early today," I reply.

"Exactement," he replies and winks at me.

I like this young man he thinks like me. These junior officers usually stay with me for three or four months as part of their training but I think I'll offer Paul a permanent post here. I'm sure he'll be delighted with the opportunity because this office has quite a reputation for solving crimes.

Paul disappears outside with a notebook and pen in his hand and I see him in deep conversation with the group of ladies. After a couple of minutes one of the ladies takes the notebook and pen from him. She seems to be writing something down then she kisses Paul on both cheeks and the group disperses.

"What was that all about?" I ask when he comes back inside. "I told them Monsieur Albert is staying at a hotel in Ceret and I said I expect him to arrive here at two-thirty but I'd telephone them if there was a change of plan. They're heading for Ceret now and, by the time they check out all the hotels, your interview will be over and the office locked up."

"But he's staying in Perpignan," I reply.

"Exactement!" he exclaims.

"They will string you up on Monday, have you

thought about that?" I ask.

"Monday is my day off," he says cheekily. "I'm sure you'll be able to deal with a few women and I'm confident you'll protect me."

"Don't bank on it," I reply but I'm unable to stifle my laughter.

Twenty minutes later Michel Albert walks through the door and I'm surprised to discover that he's a very pleasant and modest man. He's of average height, slightly plump and his clothes are smart but casual. He stands with his hands in his pockets and smiles shyly at me. I lead him through to my office and pour us both a coffee. He has his black and explains to me that he's trying to lose some weight.

"The public are very unforgiving," he says. "I'm conscious that my career depends as much on my looks as my skills as a chef and I'm no longer in my twenties."

There's a moment of awkward silence then I say, "I am very sorry for your loss, Monsieur, your mother's death must have been quite a shock for you."

"Any unexpected death, particularly in tragic circumstances, is a shock," he replies. "But the truth is, I hardly knew my mother. When I was born she left me with my grandmother and, apart from a card once a year on my birthday, I had little contact with her. She did visit me when I graduated from high school, but I was embarrassed by the way she looked and I told my friends she was just a friend of the family. Her heels were too high, her skirt was too short, her makeup too much and I was a typical teenager."

I don't really know what to say to him but I understand the discomfort he felt, because I too always felt distant from my mother when I was growing up and I still feel uncomfortable in her company today.

"I discovered when I was older that my mother provided financially for my grandmother and it was she who paid for all my needs," he continues. "I didn't realise how the money was earned and at what cost until I reached the age of twenty-two and my grandmother died because then the cheques were sent directly to me. I didn't want to accept her money so I dropped out of university and got a job working in a restaurant. When you're young there are no grey areas, you see everything in black and white. It's easy to be judgemental when someone has provided for you your entire life and you haven't had to stand on your own two feet. It must have hurt her dreadfully when I returned her cheques."

"Weren't you upset that you didn't get to complete your degree?" I ask.

"Not really, I hated my course and I guess I was never destined to be a pharmacist. My mother did visit me at that time and she begged me to resume my studies. I was very cold towards her and I told her I neither needed nor wanted her help. I said I'd survived this long without her and I could continue to do so. But the truth is, all I ever wanted was to have a mother around when I was growing up, I would have given anything for that. Now it's too late. Her last memory of me is of an angry and stupid young man. Now she'll never know how much I wanted to love her and have her love me."

I feel rather saddened by Michel's account and I change the subject to more practical considerations. It takes me only fifteen minutes to give him her diary and all the necessary paperwork. I assure him I'll be in touch as soon as the investigation is over so he can arrange for the funeral and the disposal of the house.

"You said that one of her 'girls' had been murdered," he states. "Could the same person who killed her also have killed my mother?" he asks.

I think about the question for a moment before answering, "I believe Veronique was murdered because someone wanted your mother's client book and they obviously thought she had it. However, I'm unsure, as yet, about your mother's death as I still think it was more likely to be an accident."

"I do hope you're right, Officer. It's very distressing to think she might have suffered at someone's hand."

I want to bring the interview to an end so that Paul and I can lock up the office and leave, so I tell Michel we have another appointment to go to. As I walk him to the door I mention that Patricia is a great fan of his and he very kindly offers to post his latest book to me.

"I'll write a dedication 'to Patricia' inside," he says. "Please give her my phone number in Paris and, if she's ever visiting, I'll meet up with her and show her my restaurant. You've been most kind to me and I appreciate everything you're doing for my mother."

Actually, I've done nothing for his mother

except despise the old whore for causing me so much work and stress, but who am I to burst his bubble.

CHAPTER 18

I'm sitting in the garden in my favourite chair and for the first time in a long time I'm relaxed. It's mid-morning on a beautiful sunny Sunday and there's nothing and no one demanding my attention. To say that this last week has been busy and stressful would be an understatement, it has been Hell.

Ollee is lying at my feet in a deep sleep. Occasionally he twitches or his paws move as if he's running in his doggy dreams. Patricia is working on her accounts. She's the only person I know who enjoys this work. She likes to tally up how much money she makes each week. I tease her about it and I call her my little miser, but I know that's not true. She's the most generous person I've ever met and she'd give a stranger her last centime if they needed it.

A car draws up at the front of the house and from where I'm sitting I can see that Peter has arrived with some canvasses. Like Patricia, Peter is an artist and, when he visits Perpignan to buy supplies for himself, he often picks up bits and pieces for her. After a few minutes Patricia calls to me.

"Danielle, I need ten euros because I don't have enough money to pay Peter. Can I take it out of your wallet?"

"Help yourself," I call back. She can take the lot for all I care as long as I don't have to move.

After Peter leaves Patricia comes into the

garden. She's prepared a tray with homemade lemonade and slices of her cheese flan which is perfect for a light lunch. She sets the tray down on the table and I see she's clutching something in her hand.

"I didn't know you bought lottery tickets," she states. "You always said it was a waste of money."

For a moment I'm confused then I realise she's speaking about the ticket I bought last week.

"I just checked the numbers while I was on the computer and you've won a prize," she continues. "It's the smallest prize, but you've still won something."

I can't believe it. I've only ever owned two tickets and each won a prize. I think the time has come for me to own up about the first winning ticket.

"I have something to tell you, Patricia," I say. "It will probably be a bit of a shock but don't worry it'll be a good shock."

She turns to me and her expression is gravely serious.

"Don't worry. It's good news," I tell her. "Very good news," I begin, "This is actually the second lottery ticket I've ever owned. I had a ticket for a previous draw and it too won a prize."

Her face relaxes, "You mean you bought two tickets and both of them have won? I don't believe it. You're so lucky. How much have you won?"

"I won a large prize," I say trying to break it to her gently. "The money will be available in my account either late on Tuesday or on Wednesday morning. I was told on Friday it would take two working days. I hadn't planned to tell you until I saw the money in the bank but I've definitely won and I'm definitely getting it." I pause to let the first bit of information sink in. "I met up with a man from the lottery company and he took me to a bank in Perpignan to open an account while you were at the gallery."

"How much exactly have you won?" she asks excitedly.

"We've won a fortune," I reply. "The money is for both of us. We're family and we share everything."

"How much have WE won then?"

"Two hundred thousand euros," I answer. "I won a share of the top prize."

"Two hundred thousand euros," she repeats, "Are you sure?"

"Absolutely," I say.

Patricia promptly bursts into tears, "Danielle, oh Danielle," is all she can manage to say.

"I know exactly how you feel," I tell her. "That's how I felt when I heard the news. It took me a while to get used to the idea of all that cash. Don't worry, Darling, you'll soon stop crying and start laughing. I now find myself grinning like an idiot at the most inappropriate moments."

She dries her eyes and begins to laugh, "We are rich. We are truly, very rich. The money won't change us will it?"

"Only for the better," I reply, "Only for the better."

We discuss the importance of keeping the money a secret and Patricia agrees with me that nobody must find out. I'm frightened that if people know about it they'll come begging. Patricia is frightened it will make us vulnerable and people will try to rob us. But we must satisfy our need to talk about it, so we walk around our property and we tell Ollee about the money, and we tell the chickens, and the cat, and we can't help grinning at our good fortune.

CHAPTER 19

I wake several times during the night and, when I do, I can hear Patricia moving about the house. The knowledge of the money has robbed her of sleep. I know how she feels because, now that I've shared my news with her, I feel flushed with the excitement of it all over again. I'm certain, that like me, she's thinking about all of the things we can now afford to buy. We've never been extravagant and I'm sure we never will be. We love our life just as it is right now. But not having the pressure of juggling our finances to pay for everyday things will be a real boon.

When I get out of bed in the morning and go downstairs I switch on the television to catch the early news. The newsreader's last item is an announcement that the final winner of the lottery has come forward but the person wishes to remain anonymous. That's me, I think, I am that winner and I feel a rush of excitement all over again.

I leave the house as quietly as I can because Patricia seems to have finally fallen asleep. As I drive to work I feel absolutely wired. No matter what I said to Patricia last night, having money does change the way you feel and I'm stronger and more confident now that I'm rich. Before, I never understood the attitude adopted by wealthy people, but now I do. Having money makes you sure that your opinions are the right ones.

My colleague has opened up the office and when I arrive I see there's a small group of women at the door. He's trying to placate them but they are not happy. This is obviously the fallout from Paul's actions on Saturday and, of course, today is his day off. I manage to calm the situation down by telling them Michel Albert had a change of plan at the last minute and didn't visit here or Ceret but instead stayed in Perpignan. I tell them Paul was unaware of the change of plan as he had to leave early. This seems to appease them.

I had planned to interview Raymond Dupree this morning but my colleague tells me that the hospital have been in touch and Officer Dupree has had some sort of mental breakdown. He is to be observed for another forty-eight hours then they'll report back to me. In the meantime he's to have no visitors.

There has been limited news from the forensic people but they've advised us that they managed to retrieve skin from under Veronique's fingernails. They'll be looking at this and other samples to try to identify her attacker. They've also entered Madame Henriette's house for another more detailed look. They've requested DNA samples from Dr Poullet, the two paramedics who were present on the day the body was discovered, Raymond Dupree and me so they can rule us out of the enquiry. This doesn't necessarily rule out Raymond as a suspect but he's an unlikely perpetrator of the crime. The truth is they'll find DNA samples at Madame Henriette's house from half the men in town, so it's probably a waste of time.

It doesn't take very long for the word to get out about Veronique's murder and the town is awash with rumour and speculation. It comes as no surprise when Marjorie telephones to tell me her husband is in Monpellier and he's been there for a few days. She explains he's attending a conference in his capacity as Mayor so he was nowhere near the house where Veronique lived at the time of her attack.

"I know you told me not to worry, Danielle," she says. "But this is such a terrible crime that everyone is nervous. The husbands are terrified of being exposed as clients or worse, accused of the crime, and the wives are walking about like ghosts. They are frightened to talk to each other in case they give something away."

"I fully understand, Marjorie," I reply. "Don't upset yourself because I can assure you your husband is safe. Nobody knows anything about his personal life and I will make sure that remains the case. The person who committed this crime is a violent sadist and I believe he's probably killed before. Your husband cried his eyes out for two days when his dog died, so he's hardly a candidate for this crime."

"Bless you, Danielle. Thank you for your kindness. I feel so much better now. Do you think this man might also have killed Hortense Henriette?"

"I'm still not convinced that Madame Henriette was murdered. Her death was probably an accident but only time will tell," I reply.

"Our town and, in fact, the whole surrounding area was always so quiet. What's happened to us? Why are these shocking crimes happening here?" she asks.

"I think the incomers, and the British in particular, have a lot of influence on crime levels. These people have failed in their own country and now they bring their problems to France. Also the internet and television portrays violent crime as normal. So what chance do we have?"

"It's really shocking, Danielle, I wouldn't want your job these days. We're very lucky to have you here because you're a strong and clever young woman and you always manage to solve these terrible crimes."

I'm flattered to receive such high praise from such an important lady and I thank her. She tells me, in confidence, that her husband is planning to put me forward for the award of 'Citizen of the Year' and I'm thrilled. It's a very high honour but one I believe I deserve. Patricia will be so proud if I receive this award and now she'll be able to afford to buy a new outfit for the ceremony.

CHAPTER 20

After I finish my conversation with Marjorie I receive a call from one of the stallholders who is at the small market in the square. She tells me an incident is taking place and it is getting out of hand and she asks me to attend. My colleague and I immediately leave the office and make our way to the square which is only a five minute walk away. By the time we get there a crowd has gathered. In the middle of the crowd I see two men blustering and shouting at each other. They're both swinging punches but few have landed. The wife of one of the men is standing at the sidelines yelling instructions to her husband and he's endeavouring to obey her. Both men appear to be in their sixties, both are overweight and sweating profusely.

My colleague bravely ducks the swinging arms and steps into the affray. He manages to grab one of the men by the arms placing himself between him and the other man. I immediately grab the second man who is so exhausted from the heat and his exertions that I practically have to hold him up. The first man's wife is still yelling at her husband although the crowd has now stopped baying. I tell the stupid woman to shut up or I will arrest her and at last there is silence.

"Do you want to tell me what this is all about?" I ask the man who my colleague is holding. I ask him because my man doesn't have the breath to answer. The wife begins to speak before he can reply.

"I asked him, not you," I say sharply and she gives me a thunderous look.

"He has been my neighbour for sixty years," the first man begins. "We went to school together and I trusted him. But now I know he is a lying, dishonest dog. He has cheated me and stolen my money."

"How can I steal what you leant to me?" the second man asks. "You gave me the money with your own hand."

"I leant you the money to get your van fixed because you said you were a bit short this month".

"That's true," the second man says to me. "I had a lot of expense this month and my friend leant me the money. We often help each other out and the debt is always repaid."

"Look at his stall," the first man says. "He has a brand new stall. It must have cost at least six hundred euros, so why did he lie to me and tell me he needed cash? He must have come into a lot of money very quickly to be able to afford that stall. Perhaps my good friend is the lottery winner. Perhaps he didn't wish to share his good fortune with his friend of sixty years."

"Rubbish, the other says. "This stall is not mine it belongs to my cousin. He let me use it while mine is being repaired. I told you I had a lot of extra costs this month and getting my stall repaired was one of them."

"So you haven't won the lottery then? My wife thought you won and didn't want to share your good fortune with me."

Everyone stares at the wife who for the first time has stopped muttering and is silent. She looks from one man to the other then turns and walks away through the crowd without a backward glance. It seems she was the instigator of the affray.

"Can we go now?" I ask the men. "Your argument is over, yes?"

They both nod sheepishly at me and my colleague and I leave them to get on with it. As we walk away we can't stop laughing.

"That was like two fat, old pigs dancing," he says. "I've never seen anything so funny and all because of that stupid woman's accusations."

We chat and laugh as we make our way back to the office but we are brought up sharply when we arrive. Waiting for us at the door is the prostitute called Phoebe. She is wrapped in a coat and is hugging herself and shivering even though it's a very warm day.

"Are you here to see me?" I ask.

She nods a reply. She's biting her lips and her face is twitchy and nervous, it has the pasty look of a junkie although I believe she's clean and has never done drugs. I usher her into my office and I pour two cups of coffee, she chooses to have hers black and gulps down several mouthfuls of the scalding liquid. She is near to tears when she begins to speak.

"My apartment has been trashed everything is broken. All the soft furnishings have been slashed and all the cupboards and drawers have been emptied onto the floor."

"How distressing for you," I say. "Why didn't you call us to come round? You didn't need to come to the office."

"I was too frightened to hang around at the apartment in case the person came back for me. I've been staying with friends since Veronique….."

Her voice trails off, she is unable to say the words 'was murdered' and now her tears begin to flow. I hand her a box of tissues and she mops at her eyes and nose.

"Someone is looking for Madame Henriette's client book and will stop at nothing to get it. It's valuable to a criminal you see. Once the clients' identities are known they can be blackmailed."

"I thought you said there was no client book when my colleague interviewed you, but now you're saying there is one."

"I'm sorry, but I was too frightened to tell you the truth, now I'm too frightened not to say what I know. Veronique had a boyfriend named Raul, he's Algerian and he lives somewhere in the region but I don't know where. She told him about the client book and she bragged that one day it would make her a lot of money. We all hated Raul because he lived off Veronique's earnings. He's a violent man. He used to beat her when he got angry then she couldn't work for a few days because of the bruises. Madame Henriette wouldn't let him into her house. She said she didn't trust him."

She stops to catch her breath and to gulp down more coffee.

"When Madame Henriette was killed Eveline and I immediately suspected Raul had something to do with it. He was desperate to get his hands on the book.

I think when he didn't find it he went after Veronique. Now he's after me and I'm terrified. Can you help me? Can you protect me? You must warn Eveline and Eva because they too are probably at risk."

"Go back to your friend's house and stay there," I say. "You've been safe there because Raul doesn't know where you are. I'll try to get word to the other two girls and tell them to go to a safe place. Then I'll search for Raul. There's nothing else I can do at this stage. If he did indeed kill Veronique he'll probably lie low for a while. Leave me a contact number so I can get in touch with you. I'll keep you informed of everything that's going on and I'll let you know when we've brought Raul in for questioning."

My colleague writes out the girl's new statement and she signs it, then I give her my card with my mobile number on it and show her to the door. She scurries off down the street like a frightened rabbit and, as I watch her go, I wonder if she'll be the next victim.

CHAPTER 21

I do a bit of digging but I can find nothing on Raul. Then on Tuesday I try a different tactic. I search the file on Veronique Boullier and there is mention of a Raul Armin. Two years ago she made a complaint that he'd beaten her, but when he was brought in for questioning she refused to speak against him. When I pull his file up on the computer there's more of the same, many complaints but no charges. When the time came nobody was prepared to give evidence against him.

Raul Armin was born in Algeria but his father is French and his mother is Spanish, his last known address is in La Jonquera which is just over the border in Spain. If he's gone back there he might never be found as it's a melting pot of people and a real hot spot for criminals. Hundreds of trucks stop at La Jonquera every day and a person would find it very easy to get lost amongst such a transient population.

I email my findings to Perpignan so they can check his fingerprints against those found at the two crime scenes. It's hardly worth the effort because he had reason to be in both houses, so it will prove nothing. No fingerprints were found on the bloody hammer. If it's his skin under the fingernails of Veronique, he could argue that it was there as the result of passion, and not violence, as their relationship was known to be tempestuous. I'd be very happy is he simply disappeared out of my town, preferably to another country, because nothing will bring Veronique back to life and I'd rather not have to bring him in for questioning. He's such a slippery fish that it would probably be a complete waste of time. But from what I see in his file, he's unlikely to let things go. He's been questioned about extortion and assault on several occasions and, if he is after the client book, it's because he intends to use it. I think Madame Henriette's girls are in real danger but there's nothing I can do to protect them except warn them to lie low. They chose the dangerous life they lead so they must suffer the consequences of that choice.

I have a sore head from thinking about work so at lunchtime I take a walk by the river. It's quite busy with tourists and the 'curists', who are here to take the healing waters of the spa, but by the end of September things will quieten down. Being a spa town means the population swells by ten times in the summer and that has mixed blessings. We of course need the visitors and their money because without them our town wouldn't survive, but the summer months are noisy and you can never get a seat by the river or a parking place in the street.

I decide to take a walk up one side of the river then cross at the bridge and come back down the other side. When I'm in the middle of the bridge my mobile phone rings and it's with great reluctance that I answer it in case the call forces me back to the office. It's my colleague Paul. He tells me that Eva, the maid of Madame Henriette, is in the office, and she has in her possession a notebook she wants to discuss with me. I'm curious to know what it contains, so I immediately make my way back.

Eva looks even worse that she did the last time I saw her. Her face is shiny with sweat and it has erupted with angry red patches of acne. Her hair is limp and greasy and she is skin and bone. I take her through to my office and she perches on the edge of a chair.

"I have the notebook of Madame Henriette," she begins. "She gave it to me for safe keeping. She didn't want it in her house so I looked after it for her. Here it is," she says proffering a small notebook.

I take the book from her shaking hands and glance at the contents.

"Do you think it's her client book?" the girl asks, and I realise then why she was trusted with it. It's obvious that she cannot read. The book contains nothing more than financial records.

"This is exactly what I was looking for, Eva," I lie. "Well done. You can tell everyone you've handed the book into the police and it's been passed on to Perpignan. Please let people know that you couldn't read the contents. You can tell them it was in code if you like."

I sincerely hope that by saying this word will get back to Raul and he'll give up on his search for the book. It might just save the life of this girl and the lives of Phoebe and Evaline. The girl gives a nervous cough.

"Can I go now?" she asks.

I stand up and I usher her to the door and she

scuttles away like the little cockroach she is. I tell Paul about the notebook, and about my subterfuge, and he agrees with me that it was the best thing to do.

It's late in the day when my mobile rings again and when I answer it the call is from the bank manager in Perpignan. He lets me know that the lottery money is now in my new account in cleared funds. He informs me he has a bank card and temporary cheque book for me and asks if he should post them to my home. He says he's requested a PIN number for the card and it should be with me by Friday. I thank him enthusiastically and I can hardly contain my delight. Then I ask him not to post anything out as I'll pick it all up from the bank tomorrow morning. I'll take time off from the office to go in to the bank then I'll take Patricia to the swankiest restaurant in Perpignan for lunch because I can afford it. After all, it's not every day that one wins two hundred thousand euros.

CHAPTER 22

Patricia and I drive to Perpignan early in the morning so we're there for the bank opening. I tell the girl at the reception desk the reason for our visit and we're asked to take a seat for a couple of minutes. We're both nervous and excited and I find it hard to sit still so instead I pace the floor. After what seems like an endless time the manager comes out of a door behind the reception desk. He approaches us and shakes my hand. He's a tall, slim man with black hair and a handsome face. His suit is expensive looking and his shirt has a starched, just ironed look. He carries himself with an air of confidence that seems to be natural for people in his esteemed position. I hadn't noticed how he looked the first time I met him because I was too nervous. I introduce Patricia as my good friend and he invites us into his office. The room is very plush, lots of leather and polished wood and it smells very clean.

"Would you ladies like coffee?" he asks.

"No, thank you," we both say at once.

"We're going for an early lunch," I explain. "Then I must get back to work. I'm the leading police officer on a very important murder case so, as you can imagine, I don't have much time to spare," I add.

"Really," he says. "I had no idea you held such an important post. Please forgive me, but I have many police officers as customers and none of the younger officers are usually given such responsibilities. You must be very good at your job and highly regarded."

"Danielle has been promoted very quickly," Patricia answers proudly. "She is easily the best officer they have and, as well as handling high profile cases, she's responsible for training junior officers."

"I see that your friend is a real fan," the bank manager replies smiling. Patricia blushes crimson.

"You also seem very young for your position," I reply. "Every manager I've met has been over fifty and rather crusty."

He smiles slowly then says, "How kind of you to say that, I must look better this morning than I thought I did. Hair dye and Botox work wonders I'm actually fifty-eight."

Patricia and I both stare at him in jaw dropping amazement. After a moment he begins to laugh. "I'm joking," he says. "I'm forty-two, but you're right, I am young for this post."

"You look great for forty-two," Patricia says.

"As I said, hair dye and Botox. Now, to get on with business." He reaches into his desk drawer and produces a cheque book, a bank card and some forms. "If I could just ask you to sign for these," he says, placing the forms in front of me and handing me a pen. "Each form requires your signature at the bottom. They're just receipts to show you've received the cheque book and card and, as I mentioned to you before, your PIN number and printed chequebook will arrive at your home in the next day or two. I suggest you sign the card immediately," he adds.

I do as he asks and I sign the forms and the bank

card. "I won't actually be able to see the money in my account until the PIN number arrives because without it I can't get a statement from the cash machine," I say. I'm slightly disappointed.

"Allow me," he says and he turns his computer screen so that I can see it, then he types in a reference. Immediately my account details are displayed on the monitor and both Patricia and I stare at the magic number of 200,000 euros. "When we leave my office my assistant will give you a paper copy of this statement then you can look at it whenever you like. I know I'd want to look at it all the time if I had that kind of money in my account," he adds kindly.

With the business complete he shows us out of his office then stops at one of the teller's desks to pick up the printed statement for me. Then he hands me his business card.

"If you ever have any questions regarding your account, or if you would like advice on investments, please don't hesitate to contact me," he says.

I thank him then we leave the bank. We are barely out of the door before Patricia hugs me and chants, "We are rich, rich, rich. We are so rich."

"Hush," I say. "Someone might hear you." she immediately shuts up, covers her mouth with her hand, and glances around fearfully. I'm sorry I've curbed her enthusiasm, so I put my arms around her and give her shoulders a squeeze. "We're rich, rich, rich, so very rich," I whisper in her ear.

"And no one will ever know," she adds conspiratorially.

CHAPTER 23

We have a couple of hours before lunch so we wander about the shops staring at all the things we can now afford to buy. From time to time Patricia reads a price tag or fingers a fabric but in the main she's lost in her own thoughts. We hardly speak because we can't stop thinking about the money. Designer's names which are familiar from television or newspaper adverts suddenly spring out at me from the shelves and rails, Chanel, Gucci, Moschino they are all here enticing me to buy them. Patricia loves handbags and she spends quite a long time fingering an offering by Armani.

"Would you like me to buy that for you?" I ask. "We can afford it now".

"Thank you, Danielle," she replies, flashing me one of her marvellous smiles. "But I'll refuse your kind offer because, much as I love the bag, I'd never use it. It's just not suitable for the simple life I live. I love the life we have right now and I don't need designer handbags to make me happy."

That is so true, I think to myself, she would much rather have an orchard than a designer handbag and I feel warm inside at the thought of presenting her with Monsieur Gainsboro's land.

We're not sure where to eat but we eventually settle on a smart, modern looking restaurant near the centre of town. When we enter through the heavy glass door there is a desk with a sign requesting that we please wait to be seated. A rather stiffly starched looking gentleman approaches us.

"Mesdames," he says. "Do you have a reservation?"

I look around at the empty tables, "No," I reply.

He gives me a sneer. Pretentious jerk, I think.

"I'll have to check the book. You should have made a reservation."

"You don't look very busy," I observe.

"That's because it's early and most of the people who usually dine here have already made their reservations," he replies snootily.

He spends a long time pondering the ledger in front of him, flicking pages forward and back and I'm beginning to think he's simply waiting for me to give him money to find us a table. I'm getting increasingly annoyed by his behaviour but it is Patricia who finally says something.

"It's obvious to me," she begins, "That you don't know who my friend is. I would have thought that someone in your position would recognise important people who choose to dine here. We're usually shown to the best table immediately, but if you're too busy for us we'll find another restaurant, somewhere where the staff will treat us with the respect we deserve."

His attitude immediately changes, "But of course I'll find you a table, Madame," he says. "At this time of year we're so busy with tourists, I assure you that I meant no offence."

"I've changed my mind," Patricia replies. "I

wouldn't want to eat here even if the meal was free". She grabs my arm and marches me out of the door leaving the waiter dumbfounded. "How dare he treat us that way, stuck up shit," she says. "He forgets that he's there to serve us and not the other way round."

"You were amazing, simply amazing," I say. "Where shall we eat?" I ask.

"Somewhere where the staff will treat us with the respect we deserve. How about Macdonald's?" she replies laughing, "I could murder a burger and fries."

That's my girl I think, no false airs and graces about her.

After lunch I drop Patricia back at the house and go into work. Paul presents me with a list of three names and he asks me to return their calls. One is from Marjorie so I telephone her first. When I speak to her she asks me about the book Eva found. It's apparent to me that the word is out and it has spread like wildfire. I assure her not to worry and I explain to her why I'm allowing people to think it's the client book. She's very relieved, thanks me profusely, and then ends the call quickly explaining she's late for a hairdresser appointment.

Next I telephone Monsieur Autin who is a member of the Commune Committee. The Committee are a group of privileged individuals who make most of the major decisions for our town.

"Thank you for returning my call, Officer," he begins. "I wish to discuss a rather delicate and private matter."

Having just spoken to Marjorie I think I know

what's coming, so I assure him of my strictest confidence and discretion.

"It's about the book of Hortense Henriette," he says. "I think my name might be written in it. I'm ashamed to say I was being blackmailed by her. I'd been giving her twenty euros every week for over a year, so I have to say I was relieved to hear of her death. If my wife or my colleagues, or indeed anyone in town, ever finds out I'll be ruined. What do you advise me to do?"

"I advise you to do nothing, Monsieur," I reply. "Your name is not in the book I was given. Unless you wish to try to recover the money that's been extorted from you of course, in which case you'll have to make a statement."

"No, no I'll forget about the money, it's of no consequence now. Thank you Officer, thank you so much. I'll not forget your kindness or your discretion. There's been a suggestion that you should be given a 'Citizen of the Year' award and I want you to know you'll have my full support in this matter. You deserve every accolade that this town can bestow."

He rants on and on. The relief is making this usually austere man talk rubbish and I have a struggle to get him off the phone. When I telephone the third caller, Doctor Beauchamp, it's much the same. He too had been blackmailed by Madame Henriette. When I was a child Doctor Beauchamp was always nicknamed Doctor Kinky Boots although I didn't know why, but after my conversation with him, all was revealed and I'm sorry I now know the truth.   I expect I'll be receiving many more calls over the next few days. So many wives betrayed by so many weak men, I think. I'm glad my life is uncomplicated, Patricia would never betray my trust and I would never betray hers.

CHAPTER 24

When I eventually finish my calls to the wayward men of the town, Paul tells me he's been informed that Raymond Dupree is being released from hospital tomorrow. I'm pleased that I'll be able to interview him before my day off on Friday. This is the weekend when I'm going to the grape harvest with Patricia. She's really looking forward to seeing her friends Frederick and Anna again, so I don't want anything to get in the way.

I can't say I'm particularly looking forward to the backbreaking work, but it looks as if Saturday will be the final day of picking and there's to be a party when the work is over. The best part about the harvest is the marvellous, relaxed, friendly atmosphere. Ollee is also invited which is great news. We couldn't have left him on his own for the whole weekend and it might have been awkward finding someone to take care of him. The cat, on the other hand, will fend very well for herself as long as she's left food and water. She comes and goes through the cat flap whenever she likes and she treats us like a hotel anyway. Our nearest neighbour has agreed to feed the chickens in exchange for the eggs they produce while we're away.

It's nearing the end of the day when I receive a call from Monsieur Gainsboro asking me if I can meet him at the notaire on Monday afternoon to sign the 'compromis de vente'. He says I must bring a cheque to cover ten percent of the purchase as a deposit and a further ten percent for fees. He tells me that if the land is to be in Patricia's name, she too must attend the meeting and he hopes that won't spoil the surprise. I ask him to say nothing to Patricia in the meantime because I'd prefer her to be kept in the dark until I choose my moment. At the close of day I lock up and make my way to the town centre with the intention of visiting the 'chocolaterie'. Hand made chocolates cost a fortune but they're delicious and Patricia particularly loves violet creams. Usually she buys only three or four chocolates and she rations them so she can make the experience of eating them last as long as possible, but today I intend to buy a big box.

    As I turn into the street where the shop is situated I see my mother and father walking down the hill towards me on the opposite side. I have little contact with my mother because she cannot forgive me for living when my beloved brother died. It's as if she blames me for the meningitis that robbed him of his life. She's considered to be a pious woman, but I know she confesses to the priest every week about her anger at God for taking him. I was just a child when he died and my young life was scarred by the loss of my brother and the blame my mother bestowed on me. She's a cold woman and sometimes she was very cruel. My father, on the other hand, is a gentle, sweet man but he'll always support my mother and he'll always take her side over mine. When Mama notices me she immediately rushes into the fruit shop leaving my father standing alone on the pavement outside. I cross the road and greet him.

"Hello, Papa," I say. "How are you?"

"I'm okay, Danielle," he replies. "I've been hearing all about you and the work you're doing. Everyone is saying how good you are at your job. I'm very proud of you. I hope you know that," he pauses and he looks at me with sad eyes. "I'm sorry I haven't seen you for a while but you know how it is with your mother."

He looks older and more tired than the last time I saw him. His skin looks grey and his face is puffy. I'm worried about him. My father was always such a robust man and I think the strain of living with my mother and her bitterness is taking its toll on him.

"I know what Mama's like, please don't get upset," I reply.

"How's Patricia?" he asks. "I hear her business is doing well and she's becoming very well known for her painting."

"That's right, Papa. Everyone loves her pickles and pies and her paintings are being sold at galleries in Perpignan and Narbonne."

"So you're happy in your home and you have enough money?"

Now that I'm an adult and independent I look at my father with fresh eyes. Even though he is overworked and exhausted, and his money is always hard to come by, I know he'd find a way of helping me financially if he thought I needed it. My heart breaks for the lost years we should have spent as a happy family. I'm sorry this kind man has been denied the joy of family life that should have been his by right. I can never forgive my mother for stealing this from him with her sharp tongue and impossible standards.

He keeps glancing nervously into the shop and I know my mother will remain inside until I leave. I kiss my father on the cheek and I feel my eyes fill with tears, so I say a hasty goodbye and go back across the road before I'm overcome with emotion.

When I look at the life I experience now, compared to the mere existence I had before, I realise it is contentment and not money that makes you rich.

CHAPTER 25

The decision to release Madame Henriette's body for burial has finally been made. After much coming and going between here and Perpignan there's no longer any reason to postpone it. All of the evidence points to her death being an accident and indeed, had it not been for the murder of Veronique leading us down a different path, the incident would be completely over. I've been asked to keep the file open just in case the other investigation throws anything up, but in my opinion the deaths are completely separate.

I make a telephone call to the mobile number of Michel Albert and I wake him up. He explains to me that in Paris restaurants stay open late into the night and he's only had about five hours sleep. After apologising for my faux pas, I give him the good news that he can now arrange to bury his mother and he's delighted.

"Every day the waiting drags on there is a chance of the newspapers getting hold of the story about her," he explains. "I am about to launch a new bistro in London and that kind of publicity I can do without."

"You are not responsible for your mother's indiscretions," I say.

"I do know that," he answers. "But the press is a law unto itself and very unforgiving, I am sure her lifestyle and tragic death would make lurid reading. I would like everything to be very low key," he continues. "Would you be able to advise me how to go about making the arrangements?"

"My friend Patricia used to work for the funeral director and she knows exactly what to do when it comes to funerals. Would you like me to ask her about it?"

"Better still," he says, "I would like to hire your friend to make all the arrangements for me. I would of course pay her for her help. Do you think she would agree to that? I'd like to be able to come down just for the day of the actual funeral then return to Paris without anyone knowing anything about it."

"I'm sure that Patricia will help you," I reply and I give him her phone number so he can speak to her directly.

As soon as I hang up the phone I call Patricia to warn her that Monsieur Albert will be calling her and she's very excited by the news.

"How much should I charge him?" she asks. "I'd help him for free, but I think he'd rather pay something so he can separate himself from the whole thing. It'll be easier for him to deal with it if he sees it as purely a business deal."

"I would charge him five hundred euros," I suggest, "Because that's not a large sum to him. Making these arrangements will take your time away from your own business so you should be compensated."

"The money just keeps rolling in doesn't it?" she observes happily. "I've got everything ready for our trip to the vineyard tomorrow," she says changing the subject. "I've packed a sleeping bag for each of us, just in case."

I don't like the sound of the 'just in case', but I say nothing to upset her as she's in such a happy mood and I don't want to spoil it.

After I finish the call I telephone the home of Raymond Dupree and I speak to his mother. The stupid woman just can't stop crying.

"I'm so ashamed," she sobs, "How could he let me down like that? Imagine what my friends and neighbours will be saying. We'll probably have to move now and I've lived in this house all my life."

It seems to me, she's more upset about gossip mongers than about her son having a breakdown. She's exactly like my own mother, I think, and I feel rather sorry for Raymond. I arrange to call round and interview him at two o'clock and Madame Dupree begs me not to speak to any of her neighbours. As if I would. I tell her she mustn't be present in the room when he's interviewed. She assures me she won't be in the house because she'll be in church praying for his soul. I'm right she is just like my mother. Heaven help Raymond. No wonder he sought love elsewhere.

I make one more call, this time to the notaire. He confirms that Patricia will need to be present on Monday. I'm disappointed but it cannot be helped. I'll just have to give her the surprise on Sunday before the appointment. Thinking about it gives me a warm feeling inside and I rehearse different ways of telling her the news. I decide to treat myself to lunch at the café and before I leave the office I place a large pile of files on Paul's desk.

"You're in charge," I tell him.

Laurent, the other young officer who's working with me, is not happy because he and Paul are of the same rank and both joined me at the same time. However, that's where the comparison ends. Paul is intelligent and witty and he'll go far but Laurent is a plodder and he'll remain little more than a parking attendant for the rest of his working life.

"What am I to do with these?" Paul asks tapping the files with his pen.

"Read them, write reports and file them," I answer.

"But I thought I was in charge," he says.

"You are," I reply.

With that he stands and lifts the files then drops them on Laurent's desk. "Deal with these please," he says.

Laurent's jaw drops and he looks crestfallen. He's about to protest, but Paul and I fall about laughing, so instead, he clamps his mouth shut and opens the first of the files proving my previous assessment of him.

"Enjoy your lunch, but don't drink too much Boss, remember there's a lot of work to do today," Paul says cheekily.

"Don't push your luck boy," I reply. "Everyone is dispensable."

He gives me a chastised look. He's not quite sure how far he can go with his banter and it's better he feels that way. After all, I'm the boss and he must never make the mistake of thinking he's my friend.

CHAPTER 26

When I ring the bell at the Dupree residence the door is immediately opened a small crack and Madame Dupree peers out. After identifying who's there she ushers me inside the house. I see she's already holding her handbag and as I enter she leaves and pulls the door shut behind her. The hallway is dark and the only light source is a small lamp on the hall table. The doors into the rooms of the apartment are open. Light would normally flood in from the windows, particularly on a sunny day like today, but the heavy wooden shutters outside the windows are closed causing an eerie darkness.

"Mother doesn't want anyone to know I'm home," Raymond says nodding towards the shuttered windows. "She's ashamed of me," he states. "I'm ashamed of myself, but not for loving Veronique, I'm ashamed I couldn't save her".

He offers me a seat in an overstuffed armchair and I sit down and rest my notebook on my knees. Raymond is pacing the floor in a very agitated state. He's wringing his hands and muttering to himself, his face has an exhausted clapped-out look and his skin is grey.

"Please sit down, Raymond," I say, his pacing is beginning to get on my nerves. "This won't take long. I know you've had an awful experience and I can't even begin to comprehend your loss."

"That's just it," he says. "I've just lost the love of my life. She's been stolen from me in the most violent way. He broke her beautiful fingers and her toes. Did you know that? Can you imagine what she went through?" he sobs.

I don't know what to say to him, he's distraught and I find his grief embarrassing, so I say nothing, but instead wait for him to continue.

After taking a moment to compose himself he begins, "I know Raul Armin and I saw him several times hanging about outside Madame Henriette's, but Veronique assured me it was over between them and he was at the house on other business, and I believed her. I loved her and if she'd said there were two moons in the sky, I'd have believed that as well." He stops speaking for a moment to catch his breath then he says, "When I arrived at the house on the morning of Madame Henriette's death I searched for the client book but I found nothing. Veronique told me about the book, so I knew it existed, but there was no sign of it. I assume it's been hidden somewhere off the premises. Raul must have wanted the book very badly," he says and he begins to sob again. "I'm sorry, I'm so sorry, I just can't believe that she's gone," he cries.

"Do you know where Raul lives?" I ask.

"Veronique told me he lives in La Jonquera," Raymond replies. "He's Algerian you know, but his father is French and the family has a house somewhere in the Vallespir."

"When did you last see Veronique alive?"

"Thursday afternoon," he replies. "I went to her

house because she was working there after Madame Henriette's house was locked up. She was only seeing one or two of her clients. Just to make enough money to tide her over. I asked her to give up work and marry me. She knew I loved her and we were planning where we could go if we left this place." He stops talking and swipes at his eyes with the back of his hands. "I left her at about five-thirty because I had to go home for my dinner. We were planning to meet up on Friday afternoon because, with me not working due to my suspension, I was going to take her to St Jean for a walk at the lake. When I arrived at her house the door was open and that's when I found her. Oh God, oh God, my beautiful Veronique," his voice is wracked with sobs and his shoulders are heaving with grief.

"Why did you telephone me and not the paramedics?" I ask.

He's too upset to answer me so I wait for a moment then repeat the question.

"Raymond, why did you phone me?"

"I knew she was dead," he says. His voice is flat and resigned. "She was cold and she'd probably been killed not long after I had left her. Still, I tried to revive her, even though I knew it was hopeless. I didn't want to admit she was gone and I'd never be able to speak to her again. I was in a state of total shock, still am. I had your mobile number in my phone because you gave it to me when we were dealing with Madame Henriette's death. I simply pressed the call button. I still hoped that somehow you could help me to bring her back. You're strong and clever and I was in a complete panic. I wasn't thinking straight, but I knew you'd help me."

I'm flattered by his trust in my abilities but even I can't raise the dead.

"Is there anything else you can tell me about that day? Did you speak to Veronique on Friday morning?"

"No, I didn't. I knew what the arrangements were so there was no need. She would have married me you know. She did love me."

You, Raul and half the men of the town as well, I think. Why are these men so stupid? They're paying for sex. How can they possibly think there's any love involved? They're cash machines nothing more.

I don't think I'm going to get any useful information from Raymond because he knows nothing, so I close my notebook and put it away.

"Are you feeling better now you're home?" I ask politely.

"I hate being in this house," he states. "I'm so alone now Veronique has gone and I feel these walls are closing in on me, but I've nowhere else to go. The hospital has given me sleeping pills, but they don't help. All I can see day and night is my poor Veronique's broken body. It's a nightmare that doesn't end."

"I'm truly sorry for your loss," I say, because that's what one does say in these situations, but the truth is, I don't care a bit about a dead whore or her stupid boyfriend. I just want to get out of this dismal depressing house and get back into the sunshine.

CHAPTER 27

On Friday morning the car is packed by seven-thirty and ready for our journey to the vineyard, but as usual Patricia is fussing around. She's checking and rechecking she has all she needs for the weekend and that the chickens and the cat are okay. We're not going far. The drive will take less than an hour, assuming my poor car can make it under the strain of Patricia's stuff. We're going to be near enough for me to return here if we have forgotten anything, so I wish she'd just get a move on as I hate all this hanging around.

Patricia has packed some of her fruit pies for the party tomorrow night and they smell so good I could eat one right now. Ollee is sniffing the container, great snorting sniffs as if he believes they'll suddenly pop out of the box and into his mouth. He's slavering over the box, and it's lucky it has a lid otherwise the recipients of the pies might get a bit more to eat than they bargained for. Finally, Patricia emerges from the house and locks the door behind her and our journey can begin.

We head north towards Perpignan then drive inland to the vineyard. All around, people are in the fields picking the crops. The 'ban de vendange' was announced three weeks ago and it's a grand affair with the committee visiting every vineyard. This proclamation is made every year, it announces when the harvest should begin. The date set is sacrosanct.

Frederick's late father always used to ask the local curate to bless the harvest and the pickers after the 'ban de vendange'. Patricia tells me that Frederick has continued this tradition even though he's very short of money and had to pay the curate for the blessing. I personally think it is a waste of time and money, but then I don't have very strong religious beliefs.

The road is very quiet this early in the morning and we arrive in record time. When we pull up outside the house Anna comes out to greet us.

"Frederick is already in the field," she says kissing us both. "He's been sleeping out there with the dog for the last ten days because he's terrified of the wild boar stripping the crop. He's totally exhausted and I'm very worried about his health. I'm so glad that you're here to help us. I'm really very grateful."

"How far on are you with the harvest?" Patricia asks, "Will you get it picked in time?"

"Two more days of work should do the trick," Anna says. "Then we can relax. Bless you, bless you both for coming. Now there will be eight of us for the final two days. Once the grapes have been put into the concrete 'cuve' the rest is down to the skill of the 'vigneron' and we'll no longer be at the mercy of the wildlife or the weather."

"Where shall we put our things?" Patricia asks. "Are we sleeping in the barn?"

"No," Anna replies. "You're in the house with us. Just take your stuff inside and we can sort it out later."

When we eventually get the car unpacked we go

into the field to meet up with Frederick. I can see the vines are pruned in the goblet method without wire supports. These vines are pruned yearly and form a thick trunk then their branches grow upwards to produce the goblet shape. The fruit is only twenty four to forty inches from the ground so the picking is back breaking work. We stand at the edge of the field and Frederick runs over to us and hugs us both.

"Thank God you're here," he says. "I don't know what we'd do without your help. I just couldn't get enough pickers to work for me because I can't pay them until after the wine is sold."

He looks shattered and I can see why Anna is worried. He's so exhausted that his emotions are very near the surface and, I fear at any moment, he might break down and cry. He hands us secateurs and a plastic bucket then he quickly explains the method of harvesting.

"You use the secateurs to cut the bunch of grapes from the vine then you put the grapes into the plastic bucket. Once your bucket is full you empty it into the trailer which is being pulled behind the tractor. Please be very careful because it's very easy once you begin to tire to mistake your finger for a branch. I did this when I was twelve."

He holds up his left hand and we can see that he is missing part of a finger so we heed his words. Our fellow 'vendangeurs' consist of an elderly couple who own a nearby smallholding and a young Irish couple on a gap year. Frederick tells us that the older pair has agreed to exchange their labour for some of the wine produced and the young couple are taking a month of free bed and board for their work.

We toil in the field for over three hours then Anna serves up a lunch which we devour. We're ravenous and I envy Ollee who has done nothing but play and sleep yet he also partakes of the lunch.

In the early afternoon the sun is at its hottest. It's difficult to achieve anything like the level of work you can in the morning when it is cooler, so we all have a rest after lunch. We lie in the field in the shade of a tree and the parched ground is like stone beneath our backs. Through the sprawling branches of the tree I stare up at the beautiful mountains. The highest peak in the Pyrenees is the Canigou and it can be seen from every part of the vineyard. There's something wonderful about this peak and Frederick tells us his father believed the mountain had magical powers.

We laze around and exchange stories then we resume the harvest mid-afternoon. We're revived from our rest, but by seven o'clock our working day is over because, although our hearts are prepared to go on, our bodies can do no more.

CHAPTER 28

Patricia and I share a very lumpy bed which is in a curtained-off area of the main living room. Anna is asleep upstairs and once again Frederick is in the field with his dog. The elderly couple have gone home for the night and the young couple are being accommodated in the barn. I fall asleep as soon as my head hits the equally lumpy pillow and I don't wake until early morning.

It's Ollee who breaks my sleep by licking my face. The dog refused to stay outside last night as the noises of the countryside and the unfamiliar surroundings upset him. We ended up having to give in to him and let him inside because his incessant whimpering and scratching at the door was disturbing everyone else.

Frederick was delighted with the work our team produced yesterday and he expects, if we do the same today, the harvest will be safely in the 'cuve' by dinnertime. I'm so glad Patricia brought hats and sun cream for us because otherwise I'd have been burnt to a crisp. The elderly couple who are working alongside us both have skin like leather. They have worked outdoors for years and their skin is dry and wrinkled and the colour of a walnut.

I turn over in bed and my body feels as if it's gone ten rounds in a boxing ring. I just hope I can keep going until the harvest is in. Patricia stirs when I move and, as I climb out of the bed, Ollee jumps onto it and smothers her face and ears with slobbering licks.

"Is it morning already?" she asks while struggling to curb the dog's enthusiasm. "Do I have to get up now?"

"I'm afraid so," I reply.

"But I'm still so tired" she moans.

"Remember that the next time you volunteer for something. At least this is our last day. The rest of them have already been working at this for over a week."

When we are dressed, we see Anna has already gone to the field, but she's left us a note asking us to help ourselves to breakfast. We eat quickly then make our way to the part of the vineyard where we're going to be working today. The others are singing as they work and my spirits are lifted by the songs. It takes me back to my childhood when I would often hear singing as I passed by the fields at harvest time. For some reason this makes me think of my father and I hope that he's well. I was worried about him when I last saw him, because he seemed frail and tired, so I make up my mind to call him tomorrow to make sure he's okay.

At precisely five-twenty-five, the last vine has been reached and the final bunch of grapes is ready to be severed from the branch. We're all tired but jubilant as Frederick, with tears streaming down his exhausted face, makes the final cut. The trailer is driven to the 'cuve' and the last of the grapes is delivered and placed inside. We all cheer and toast the grapes with a glass of wine from one of last year's bottles and Anna makes a call to her neighbour to see if they've completed their harvest.

At seven-thirty we're joined by ten other 'vendangeurs' from the neighbouring vineyard along with the owner and his wife. They are in high spirits having also completed their harvest. They arrive on the back of a truck and they bring with them trestle tables and chairs together with food and wine for the celebration. We're told, when Frederick's father was alive, it was arranged that the celebrations be held turn about between the two vineyards and this year is Frederick and Anna's turn.

As the men set up the tables the women spread crisp white linen cloths over them, then the food is laid out. We're all really hungry from the hard work and the sight of steaming cassoulets and confits makes me salivate. There's a huge range of food and, when we are seated and prayers have been said, we all tuck in. We begin with charcuterie served with a Catalan salad. This is quickly followed by the rich stews, garlic potatoes, cauliflower au gratin and ragouts. It all tastes wonderful and we gorge ourselves mopping up the gravy with chunks of fresh bread.

Everyone in the party is drinking copious amounts of wine and the songs are getting decidedly bawdy when we're presented with the desserts. We are full up from our meal but the desserts of plum clafouti, choux a la crème and Patricia's delicious fruit pies are impossible to resist. I look across the table at Patricia, her blue eyes are sparkling and she is singing and laughing. She catches sight of me looking at her and she stares into my eyes and mouths a kiss.

I don't know what time the party ended, as people either drifted away or fell asleep round the fire, but Patricia and I returned to the house well after midnight and fell asleep in the lumpy bed with Ollee snoring between us. We don't wake until lunchtime the next day then we pack up the car and reluctantly say our goodbyes. It has been a marvellous experience bringing in the harvest and, even though every bone in my body is aching, I find myself volunteering to help next year.

CHAPTER 29

As we drive home Patricia is chattering on and on about how wonderful it is to grow your own crops. She points out how much money we save because of our chickens and our kitchen garden and she's right. I love to listen to her happily making plans for the coming months. For a modern girl, her attitude surprisingly is like that of an old fashioned housewife.

"Perhaps I should plant some 'myrtille'," she says "Everyone loves the berries' mixture of sharpness and sweet and I could use them in pies and jams."

The rich blue berries are one of my favourites and I'd eat them straight off the bush if we had them.

"We've got that little piece of ground at the side of the house, the soil is always a bit damp, so that should suit them rather well," she continues.

She's so busy chatting and planning that she hasn't noticed that I've taken the road which goes past Monsieur Gainsboro's orchard and, when I reach the field, I stop the car.

"Why are we stopping?" she asks. "Oh, we're at the orchard," she observes. "Why have you stopped here, Danielle?"

"Please get out of the car," I say and she gives me a mystified look but does as I ask. We stand facing the orchard, "Everything that you see in front of you is yours," I say. "I'm buying this orchard for you Patricia."

"What? What?" are the only words she can manage to utter "Can you say that again?" she asks staring at me in disbelief.

"I said, I'm buying the orchard for you," I repeat.

"But we agreed we couldn't afford it. It costs a fortune," she replies.

"We have a fortune now with the lottery win," I point out. "We can afford it and we are going to have it. I've made an appointment for us to go to the notaire tomorrow with Monsieur Gainsboro and start the ball rolling."

"I don't know what to say. I'm lost for words."

"Well that's a first," I reply laughing.

She stands for a moment, looking out over the land then she throws her arms round me and showers me with kisses.

"If anyone asks, we must say that the bank has given us a loan. No one must know we have the money," she says, and I agree with her.

I'm enjoying the feeling of wealth and power, and I'm delighting in Patricia's excitement when my phone ring and I receive a message that my father has collapsed in the street. It's my friend Byron calling. He informs me that my father is being taken to hospital in Ceret. My heart lurches and I feel sick.

Byron is an elegant English gentleman who resides in and has business interests in my town. He's helped me enormously and he's been instrumental in me gaining the position I now enjoy. I have many acquaintances, but I count Byron as a friend.

"What's happened to him?" I ask. "Is it bad?"

"I'm not sure, Dear Girl," he replies. "I was sitting at the café having coffee and reading the Sunday papers when I saw him stagger and fall down. I called for the paramedics immediately and your friend Jean attended. I was at your father's side the whole time and he could talk coherently, he never lost consciousness, but he couldn't get up. It was as if all his strength had left him."

"But he was talking," I say. "You're sure he was talking the whole time."

"Oh yes, Dear Girl, the poor man kept apologising for being such a nuisance. I assured him he was nothing of the kind."

"Did Jean say anything to you about my father? Did he give any indication about what's happened to him?

"He didn't say anything positively, and I don't want to give you false information, but I think it might be an angina attack, because your father's colour wasn't good and his breathing was difficult. When I first went over to him, he said he had some pain in his jaw, that's often an indication of heart trouble."

By the look on my face, Patricia has realised something is very wrong. She's standing quietly beside me with a look of deep concern in her eyes. I thank Byron for calling me and he offers to accompany me to the hospital.

"I'm with Patricia," I say, "But you'd be doing me a great favour if you'd please check that my mother knows what's happened and, if necessary, bring her to the hospital."

"I'll do that right now, Danielle," he replies. "Don't you worry about a thing, just get yourself to the hospital."

I thank him and hang up then I quickly explain to Patricia what's happened. We drive to our house to drop off Ollee before making our way to the hospital. I'm worried sick and I'm angry at myself for not checking on my father when I first felt something was wrong with him.

CHAPTER 30

I park badly then run into the hospital where I see my mother standing in front of me. She looks much older than her years. Her body seems shrunken and stooped. She's dressed in her customary black shift. Her grey hair is tied back into a tight bun and the skin on her face is lined and papery.

She doesn't see me enter, "Hello Mama," I say and she turns.

She stares at Patricia and me, "What's she doing here?" she asks nodding towards Patricia. "It's not her father who's dying."

I feel the colour drain from my face, "Is Papa dying?" I ask hoarsely with fear constricting my throat.

"He might as well be, for all you care," she answers acidly.

"Mama," I plead. "Tell me, is he really that ill?"

"The doctor said he'll come and speak to me once he's finished his examination, so you'll just have to wait, unless of course you have somewhere more important to be. Your friend can go, I don't want her here," she adds spitefully.

"I can get a taxi," Patricia says. "I can see you at home, Danielle. It's important for you to be here for your parents and I don't want to upset your mother any further."

I see my mother smirk and I'm angry. She's more interested in scoring points over me than she is in my father's condition.

"Please stay, Patricia," I say, "I need you here."

"Very well," she replies. "You know that I'll always be here for you."

"Sickening perverts," my mother spits out her words. "No wonder your father is so ill, he's ashamed of you."

"My father is proud of me," I reply angrily. "He told me he's proud of me, and Patricia. I won't let you put your poisonous words into his mouth. Patricia and I are not perverts, as you well know. We simply share a house together. Papa is ill because he's been overworking."

"Pah, what do you know," she retorts. "He has not been overworking he hasn't been working at all. He was made redundant six weeks ago and he's worried sick. He's been walking the streets every day looking for work. If you love him as much as you think you do, you'd know the terrible state he's in."

I had no idea that my father was out of work and I had no knowledge of the strain that he was under.

"We're not short of money," she continues, "So don't try giving him any handouts or you'll upset him further. It's his pride that's been damaged, because he's too old to compete for the few jobs that are available. Younger, less-skilled men are being favoured for the work and your father feels useless and helpless. Thanks to your precious job and lifestyle, he has no grandchildren to distract him from his miserable situation, and no hope of any in the future." She stares hard at Patricia and her eyes are full of hatred. Patricia shrinks under her gaze and I find myself, not for the first time, apologising to her for my mother's venomous tongue.

A doctor appears from a side room and, as he approaches us, we wait with trepidation for him to speak.

"Madame," he says addressing my mother, "Your husband will be ready for you to visit in a couple of minutes. A nurse will come and fetch you shortly. It seems to have been an angina attack, but we will know better when the test results come back in a few days. In the meantime, we'll be keeping him in for observation, but he's doing well, so don't worry."

"May I see my father, Doctor?" I ask.

"Perhaps tomorrow," he replies. "He's very tired and I think it would be better if he had only one visitor today."

I'm very upset at not being allowed to visit. My mother is smiling smugly, she's gloating with pleasure because I may not see my father, and I hate her for that.

"Thank you, Doctor," she says addressing him, her voice is sickly sweet. "I'll be very quiet and I'll only stay for a few of minutes. You've been very kind."

I'm so upset I can't speak and I storm out of the hospital without looking back. Patricia runs after me.

"Danielle, don't you think we should wait and offer your mother a lift?" she asks.

I can't understand how Patricia can still be so kind and caring after the awful way my mother treated her.

"The old witch can fly home on her broomstick, for all I care," I reply. "I can't bear to be in her company another minute."

CHAPTER 31

On Monday I telephone the hospital and I'm informed that my father's had a good night and he's feeling well. The nurse tells me when I can visit and I'm relieved I can see him later today. I need to see him for myself to be assured he's alright. When I go to the office, I change the appointment with the notaire to five o'clock, so I've time to go to the hospital.

After the upset of yesterday I find it hard to concentrate on anything else, but in truth, the only important case at the moment is the murder of Veronique. My colleagues in Spain have checked out the address I've been given for Raul Armin. They reported back to me that, not surprisingly, there is no such address. I telephone Raymond Dupree and, I'm informed by his mother, he's gone out for a walk. I ask her to get him to call me when he returns because, with a bit of luck, he'll have some idea where Raul might hang out. Mid-morning Patricia telephones and asks me how I am. She's worried because I was so upset at the hospital yesterday and I found it difficult to talk about it. I assure her I'm much better because I can see my father today.

"You do know your mother will probably be there at the same time," she says. "Will you be okay with that?"

"Don't worry, Patricia, I was very upset and frightened yesterday, but I'll be prepared for her today," I reply. "How are you? I'm sorry she excelled at being a bitch yesterday and most of her venom was aimed at you."

"Don't worry, Danielle I've being dealing with prejudice all my life. Her cruel words are like water off a ducks back to me. I've been making the arrangements for the funeral of Madame Henriette," she says, changing the subject. "I spoke to her son first thing this morning. It's taken only two phone calls for me to organise the whole thing. I feel a bit guilty to be charging him five hundred euros for a couple of calls, but he's delighted I'm helping him."

"I wouldn't feel guilty, Patricia, it might only be two phone calls for you, but it would probably have taken him much more effort. Besides, you've removed all the stress from him and that's priceless. When's the funeral being held?"

"Three o'clock on Thursday. The prayers will be said in the chapel at St Jean before the burial. By having it there, no-one will realise it's for Madame Henriette. Only the priest, Michel Albert and I, will attend the cemetery. Everything will be done and dusted within a couple of hours then Michel can go back to Paris. He's giving a sizeable donation to the chapel at St Jean, so the priest is delighted. He's assured me he fully understands the need for discretion. My old boss is supplying the coffin and the cars and flowers. He's delighted that I recommended him and he's giving me fifty euros for introducing the business."

I congratulate Patricia on her good work then I advise her of the revised time for the meeting with the notaire.

"I still can't believe this is happening," she says. "I'm going to go and look at the orchard again, right now. Monsieur Gainsboro said I can help myself to the apples so I'm taking a bag with me. You'll be having apple pie tonight with your coffee. How does that sound?"

"Marvellous, that sounds absolutely marvellous," I reply. "I'll pick you up at the house at four-thirty and we'll go and buy your orchard. 'A bientot', Darling. Have a lovely day."

After we've said our goodbyes and I hang up the phone, another call comes in almost immediately from my good friend Byron.

"Hello, Danielle," he begins and after enquiring about my father he asks, "Is it alright if I come and see you this morning? I've something I want to discuss with you. It's about the murder of the prostitute."

I'm intrigued because I can't see any possible connection between Byron and Veronique. He's just not the kind of man who would visit a whore.

"I'll put the coffee on, Byron, you bring the 'pain au chocolat'," I say. "Can you give me about half an hour? That'll give me time to clear my desk."

"Perfect, thank you, Danielle. I think what I have to tell you will interest you because it involves a police officer. I'll see you soon and don't worry I'll bring the chocolate fix with me."

Something involving a police officer, I think, now I'm really intrigued.

CHAPTER 32

The door of my room is slightly ajar and when Byron arrives at the office I can hear him engage in friendly banter with Paul.

"He better not be after my 'pain au chocolat'," I say to Byron as I go to greet him.

"No problem, Boss," Paul replies. "This kind gentleman has brought them for the whole office, so unless you're in need of a bucketful of chocolate, we're okay."

"He's a cheeky chappie, but very likeable," Byron says, as I show him into my office and shut the door.

"Yes," I agree. "I think he'll go far because he does have a very friendly manner and he's smart too. Anyway first things first, I'll pour the coffee and you put the croissants onto the plates. I've left them on my desk."

"Yes, Mam," he replies, giving me a salute. "We'll deal with the important things first, pleasure before business always."

When we're seated and eating the delicious warm croissants and sipping the good, dark coffee Byron begins to speak.

"I was in my apartment block at the weekend to collect the rents and I was surprised to receive a visitor in the shape of a police officer. He told me his name was Officer Dupree and he was based in Ceret. He had some questions regarding a man called Raul Armin. I thought it strange that he was calling on me at the weekend, without first phoning to make an appointment, and that he was coming from Ceret instead of from this office." He stops to sip his coffee then says, "He was in uniform when he called, so I know he's definitely a policeman. I'm afraid I could tell him very little. Raul did rent an apartment from me a few months ago, but it was only for a short time, then he left and said he was going to La Jonquera. The thing I thought most odd was the officer asked me to tell no-one of our conversation, not even you, Danielle. He seemed to be acting in a very strange way, so I agreed, without question, then I showed him out and locked the door behind him."

Merde, I think. Raymond Dupree is suspended and he shouldn't be in uniform or questioning anyone.

"You said he was acting strangely, Byron, in what way?"

"He looked dishevelled and he seemed out of it, as if he was drugged up. His eyes kept drifting and he was having difficulty following the conversation. I do hope I've done the right thing in coming to you."

"Absolutely," I reply. "Officer Dupree has been suspended while the investigation into the murder of the prostitute is taking place because he knew the girl intimately. I'm telling you this because I trust it'll go no further. He shouldn't be asking questions regarding the case."

"I take it Raul Armin is somehow involved," Byron says. "I personally thought that he was a piece of shit and I was pleased when he ended his tenancy. There's something dangerous about him. I'm sure he sails very close to the wind, where the law is concerned. Often, one or two of his friends would visit him and they were shifty looking as well."

"I can't really tell you much Byron, as the case is ongoing, but I can say this, if you come across Raul keep out of his way and telephone me immediately. Also, if you see Raymond Dupree, please let me know because I want to catch up with him before he gets himself into trouble."

"It sounds as if this Raymond is a very stupid man. I hope he doesn't find Raul because in a confrontation, my money would be on Raul every time."

I have to agree with Byron there Raymond wouldn't stand a chance. We finish our coffee and croissants and spend some time chatting. He's delighted when I tell him about the orchard.

"You two must be doing very well to be able to afford it," he says.

"Bank loan," I reply. "I'll be paying it for the rest of my life."

"The bank owns us all," Byron replies. "Now there's a business I should be in."

I'm about to show Byron out when I hear a commotion coming from the main office, so I leave him seated and go to see what's going on. The whore called Evaline has come into the office. She's shouting at Paul and showing him her arm which is in a plaster cast.

"Get out of my way," she says when she sees me and she shoves him roughly. "I want to speak to the organ grinder not the monkey."

Seeing what's occurring through the open door, Byron swiftly stands and comes out of my office. He calls a 'goodbye' to me and leaves hastily. I usher the very upset Evaline into my room and close the door. I have to leave for the hospital in half an hour and, by the look on Evaline's face, this might take considerably longer.

CHAPTER 33

"He did this," Evaline says holding up her arm. She has not taken a seat yet. "He did this. That madman fractured my wrist."

"Please sit down," I say, but she doesn't move. She's standing and glaring at me. "Sit down and tell me calmly exactly what has happened to you," I repeat.

She paces the floor, then with a sigh and a sulky look, she throws herself down on the chair and begins, "I was staying with a friend in Le Boulou after you warned me to lie low, only the police were aware of my address in case you needed to get in touch with me. I was walking in the street at about eleven o'clock last night when somebody came up behind me and grabbed my arm. I got the shock of my life because I immediately thought of Raul. I would have screamed, but he clamped his other hand over my mouth. I thought I was going to be mugged, or worse."

She stops talking and takes cigarettes and a lighter from her bag and proceeds to light up. I reach behind me to lift the ashtray from the worktop and I place it in front of her on the desk. She draws on the cigarette then exhales loudly and continues.

"Imagine my surprise and relief when the man speaks into my ear and says that it's Raymond the cop. He was a client of Veronique. He says he'll take his hand from my mouth but I mustn't scream and I nod my head in agreement." She puffs again at her cigarette. "He wants to know where Raul is and I tell him that I'm hiding from him and I have no idea where he is, but Raymond doesn't believe me. He's holding my wrist tightly and he's hurting me."

She begins to shake and her voice trembles with emotion. "Two men are walking along the street and they call over to me and ask me if I'm okay. Raymond says he's the police and unless they want to be involved in a soliciting charge they should walk on. They rush away and leave me with him. I'm really frightened now and I try to get away but Raymond is holding my wrist tightly. He pulls me and twists my arm and I hear a crack and the pain in my wrist is excruciating."

She's now sobbing, her eyes are streaming and mucus drips from her nose as she puffs again on her cigarette. I hand her a box of tissues and she takes some out and mops her face. She sits quietly weeping for a moment before continuing.

She takes a deep breath to steady herself, then says "I'm sitting on the pavement crying and I'm begging him to let me go, the pain in my arm is so bad that I vomit onto the road. It's then he sees what he's done and he offers to take me to the hospital. I just want to get away from him, so I tell him my friend will help me. Then he looks down at me and, cool as a cucumber, he says, 'keep in touch' then he walks off down the street leaving me on the ground. Can you believe it?" she says. "He asks me to keep in touch."

I'm totally shocked by what Evaline has told me. Raymond must have been given her address from the office in Ceret. Someone has given him these confidential details while he's on suspension and, from what Evaline has said, it sounds as if he's heading for a complete breakdown.

"Do you want to press charges?" I ask praying she says no.

"Don't be stupid," she replies sharply. "Can you imagine what my life would be like if I did that? Every policeman in the region would have it in for me. I can't work for the next month because of this," she says holding up her cast. "If I rat on a cop I might as well hang up my corset and stockings for ever because I'd never work again."

I assure her I'll track Raymond down and he'll be punished for what he's done then I ask Laurent to drive her home. When they leave I tell Paul what's happened.

"Bloody hell the stupid prick has gone too far this time," Paul says. "I hope he has gone mad, because otherwise they'll throw the book at him."

"We must keep this quiet and find Raymond before he injures himself or anyone else," I say. "He is a colleague after all and the whore doesn't want to press charges. Put the word out that when he's found he must be held until I speak to him."

When I leave the office I have just enough time to make it to the hospital to see my father. My head is thumping and the day is disappearing rapidly, what a mess I think, what a bloody mess.

CHAPTER 34

I break the speed limit most of the way and arrive at the hospital on time for my visit. Parking is a bitch, as usual, but I eventually manage to squeeze my car into a small space between a recycle bin and a fence. It's at times like this I wish I had a smaller car, but as much of the area I cover is in the mountains, a four wheel drive is essential for my work.

As I enter the hospital I glance around nervously but see no sign of my mother. I'm relieved but upset at the same time. Surely she'll come to visit my father today? I scan the people in the entrance hall again, but she's definitely not here. Perhaps she's already in the ward. I head for the ward and, with each step, I expect to see her. It fills me with trepidation. I don't know why she has the ability to make me feel like this, I'm a grown woman now and no longer the little girl she used to belittle.

My father is in a ward with three other men and, when he sees me enter the room, he waves at me and smiles, all the other men have visitors. He's the only one with nobody by the bedside. He looks small and shrunken in the hospital bed and his pyjamas are old and threadbare.

"Hello, Papa," I say and I lean over to kiss his cheek. "How are you?"

"I'm fine, Danielle. Don't be alarmed by this machine," he says indicating to a monitor. "I'm to be attached to this thing for twenty-four hours so they can monitor my heart. It's just strapped to me, I haven't any tubes or wires so don't be afraid. Your old Papa is not ready to depart from this world just yet, besides your Mama wouldn't let me go, I haven't yet served my sentence."

I'm very relieved that he's well enough to make jokes with me, but I find the reference to his life with my mother very poignant and I fill up.

"There, there, Danielle," he says taking my hand in his and patting it gently. "Please don't be upset, I'm really okay. They'll let me out in a couple of days and I'll be as right as rain."

"Where's Mama? Isn't she visiting you today?"

"She knew you would visit and it's difficult for her without a car, but she'll telephone to see how I am later."

"But Papa, she knows I'd pick her up and drive her here. Why didn't she call me?"

"Danielle, you know how she is," he answers with a grimace. "She doesn't want to be beholden to anyone."

"She doesn't want to be beholden to me, you mean," I reply.

"So how is Patricia," he says changing the subject.

"She's fine Papa, we're both fine, in fact we're doing really well. Mama told me about your job and I'm really sorry. You'd been with that company for so long."

"That's the truth," he replies. "Most of us had

been with the company for years, but these are hard times and they simply don't have the business, so they've cut the staff by forty per cent."

"You must be near retirement, Papa, couldn't they have let you work until then?"

"They tried to hold on, but they simply ran out of orders and money. They might still go under, even with the changes they've made. But you're right I had only thirty weeks to go."

I knew it was near but I didn't realise that my father was so close to retirement, thirty weeks was nothing.

"It's not the money, Danielle, your Mama and I will manage. It's having no job to go to that's so depressing. I hate this feeling of being all washed up. When you're retired it's okay to be seen walking in the street in the middle of the day because it's your right after working all your life, but when you're unemployed, you're ashamed not to be working."

"You've nothing to be ashamed of Papa. There are many men walking the streets who have never worked and have no intention of ever working. They're the ones who should be ashamed."

"I can't change my nature, Danielle, and I can't help the way I feel. Anyway, let's not talk about it any more. Let's talk about you and Patricia. What's new?"

I tell my father about the orchard that we're going to buy and he's delighted for us.

"When I was a young man I used to do farm work and, funnily enough, one of my first jobs was tending an orchard," he tells me. "There's quite a lot involved in the management of the trees. They need constant care and attention to get the most out of them."

"We know nothing about running an orchard, Papa. Perhaps when you're better, you could help us?"

"It would be my pleasure, Danielle. It's not as if I am doing anything else at the moment."

His words put a thought into my head and I find myself speaking aloud. "I have a great idea, Papa, if you don't mind working for minimum wage until you retire. I can employ you to look after the orchard. I'll pay you minimum wage and I'll pay the contributions, so you'll get all your benefits when you reach retirement age. In return, you can teach Patricia how to look after the orchard and help her with all the work. It's a win, win situation all round."

"It's very kind of you, Dear, but even at minimum wage, for a full weeks work with contributions, you'd be paying about three hundred euros a week for thirty weeks. That's about nine thousand euros."

"Papa, it's a small price to pay for the knowledge we'll be gaining. Once we know what to do, we'll reap the benefits for years to come, and besides, once the thirty weeks is up, I'll expect you to volunteer your work in return for some of the fruit. So we'll get an employee that costs us nothing after the first thirty weeks. I have money, Papa, as I said Patricia and I are doing very well and you know that I was promoted recently, the promotion came with a very large salary increase."

I can see he's thinking about my suggestion

and I know that I've offered this without consulting Patricia, but I'm sure she won't object. I hadn't realised that owning an orchard isn't just a matter of picking the fruit. I really hope my father accepts my offer.

"Please help me, Papa. Please say yes because I'm investing a lot of money in this orchard and I don't want to lose it because of our ignorance."

"Your Mama won't like it," he replies.

"Do you need Mama's permission to help your daughter?" I ask.

"No, of course not. Thank you, Danielle, I will accept your kind offer of work. When do I start?"

"I'm signing the 'compromis de vente' later today with a view to completing the deal as soon as possible. How about giving yourself one month to recover, but I'll employ you immediately, so I'll pay the contributions from tomorrow, I just won't pay you any wages until you actually start the working. Does that sound fair?"

"That's more than fair, Danielle. During the first month, when I'm not physically working, I'll consult with Patricia and advise her about what tools she'll need. I can look at the orchard to see the state of the trees and see if there is room for more planting."

My father is very animated and enthusiastic about the project and he's regained the twinkle in his eyes. The money is a small price to pay for his health and wellbeing and with his help the orchard is more likely to be a success. However, I'm really pleased that it is he and not me, who has to tell my mother.

CHAPTER 35

After my visit with my father I head back to the office to see is there's any news about Raymond, but unfortunately Paul has been unable to locate him. I don't think I can rely on him to return to his mother's house, and I can't leave him out there any longer, given his state of mind, so I alert all the police stations in the region to look out for him. I tell them he's had a mental breakdown and there's a risk he may harm himself. I don't mention that he might also be a risk to Raul Armin because, quite frankly, I don't give a damn about him. Afterwards, I contact the hospital and speak to a Doctor Nundy, who was in charge of Raymond's assessment and treatment and, when I tell her he's missing, she immediately goes on the defensive.

"I had no reason to detain him," she says. "Yes, he was depressed, but given the circumstances, who wouldn't be? I gave him anti-depressants and they should keep him calm, so I'm not too worried about him."

"He broke a girl's arm and he's searching for a murder suspect so he can confront him, if that doesn't worry you what on earth will?" I say sarcastically.

"I don't like your tone of voice, Officer," Doctor Nundy replies. "When you do get in contact with Raymond, please ask him to come in for another assessment and I might consider changing his medication."

"You don't like my tone of voice," I say. I'm

outraged by her reply. "Well I don't like your manner, Doctor Nundy, and, if I do come across Raymond, you'll be the last person I tell."

"You are very rude, Officer. I have nothing more to say to you. I'll be complaining to your superiors."

"I am the superior, Doctor Nundy. I'm in charge of this investigation, so complain all you like. I can assure you, I'll give you the same amount of attention that you gave Raymond Dupree."

Before I can say any more she hangs up. Stupid woman, I think, by letting Raymond home without a proper assessment she has set a bomb ticking that nobody knows how to diffuse.

There's nothing else I can do at the moment except wait for Raymond to turn up, so I leave Paul to lock up and I drive home to collect Patricia. I've a lot to tell her about my father and I hope she'll see my offer to him as a positive thing. When I enter the house the delicious aroma of warm apples and sugar tantalises my senses and Patricia rushes over to me and hugs me.

"This is so exciting, Danielle," she says. "I'm all ready for the visit to the notaire."

"Something smells good" I say.

"That smell is our apples picked from our trees. Isn't it wonderful?"

"So you visited the orchard today and you're still happy about it? You're sure you want to go ahead?"

"I'm ecstatic, I'm thrilled and I'm every other word you can think of for delighted," she replies. "I didn't realise just how large the orchard is, it's amazing. There will be a lot of work involved but I'm sure I'll manage. I really don't know much about trees, but I'll pick it up, because I've a lot of energy and I'm a very fast learner."

Her statement gives me the opportunity to tell her about my father and her reaction is just what I'd hoped for.

"How wonderful, Danielle," she says. "Your father will be able to teach me how to run the orchard to get the most out of it, and we, in turn, will help to restore his self esteem. The added bonus is that you'll be able to spend time with him without having to put up with your mother. You can be damn sure she won't step foot in the orchard, so both you and your father will get a break."

I hadn't thought of that aspect of the arrangement, but Patricia is right, my mother won't come near the place and my father will get some peace.

I realise I've had no lunch so I have a slice of apple pie and a mug of coffee then we head off for the notaire's office. I intend to pay the deposit from our joint bank account rather than the new account then transfer the money later, so as not to draw attention to it. Then, when it is due, I can pay the balance by bank draft.

When we arrive we're shown into a room that has little in it except for a large table surrounded by chairs. There is one tiny window to the side and the room is very small. Certificates showing various qualifications that the notaire has obtained hang on the walls. The notaire is seated at the head of the table and Monsieur Gainsboro is seated to the right of him. As we enter both men stand and everyone shakes hands formally. The secretary enters the room carrying a bundle of blue cardboard files which she places on the table then she closes the door behind her and we all sit down. This is the same office that Patricia and I were in to sign the papers for our house purchase and I have a pleasant feeling of de ja vu.

The proceedings take about half an hour, but it feels much longer because I'm so anxious to conclude the bargain. The notaire has to ensure that everyone understands the contract and is happy with it. We have to initial every page of the agreement then sign the final page. After I hand over the cheque the notaire congratulates us and Monsieur Gainsboro kisses Patricia and me on both cheeks.

We are advised of the cooling off period which gives us time to change our minds, but we both give our assurances to Monsieur Gainsboro that this won't happen. Finally, we can leave the notaire's office and we drive home to celebrate.

We eat our meal in the garden and wash it down with lots of wine. I feel rather tipsy but we can't resist getting into the car and driving to the orchard for another look. Fortunately, we meet no other cars on the way and I manage to get us home afterwards in one piece. It was a stupid risk to take but sometimes common sense goes out the window when you feel so happy you could burst.

CHAPTER 36

It's Thursday morning, the day of Madame Henriette's funeral, so I drop Patricia at the funeral parlour on my way to work. I've had word from the hospital that my father is to be released today and I've arranged to collect him at eleven o'clock. Surprisingly, my mother has accepted my offer of a lift, although she's only agreed to it if I promise not to wear my uniform when I call for her. I'd wear a clown suit if it makes any difference, as long as she allows me to help my Papa.

I'm trying to clear my desk before going to pick her up, when Paul buzzes through to me to tell me that Monsieur Autin from the Commune Committee is in the outer office and he wishes to see me. I'm not sure what he wants, because I thought I'd already reassured him about Madame Henriette's client book, so I ask Paul to show him through to my office.

When he enters the room I stand and offer him my hand, "Bonjour, Monsieur Autin," I say, "Ca va?"

He takes my hand and shakes it enthusiastically, "Bonjour, Danielle, tres bien merci. Ca va et vous," he replies.

"Yes, yes I am good. How can I help you?" I ask.

"It is I who wishes to help you," he replies smiling. He hands me four white envelopes and I see from the typewritten names on the front that they're for

Patricia, my mother, my father and me.

"What's this?" I ask.

"I'm here in my official capacity from the Commune Committee and I'm delighted to inform you that you've been awarded the honour of 'Citizen of the Year'. The certificate will be presented to you at the annual town meeting next Wednesday. The invitations are for you and your family. Well done, Danielle. It's a very well deserved honour."

I'm thrilled, perhaps at last my mother will see how important my work is and how much respect I'm shown.

"Thank you, Monsieur, I'm overwhelmed."

"We all know times are changing and we're no longer the sleepy little town we once were. But with your good work and help we're fortunate that the bad things that do happen rarely touch the ordinary people of our town. This award is a very small thing compared to what you give to us, and I, and indeed the whole Committee, am delighted to bestow this honour on you. The Mayor will be presenting you with the award and I'll tell you now, there will also be a cheque for one hundred euros."

"I'll be delighted to receive the award," I say. "But I would prefer the cheque to be donated to a worthy local charity on my behalf if that's okay. I'd feel embarrassed to receive money for doing my job."

"Of course it's okay and very worthy of you. We are definitely honouring the right person," he says with a smile.

When he leaves the office I tell Paul what has

taken place. "Citizen of the year, eh?" he says. "Short of candidates were they? Go on, own up, it was between you and that idiot who cleans the streets wasn't it?"

I pick up a file from his desk and smack it off his head. "You're getting far too cheeky," I say, but I can't help laughing.

"Joking apart, Boss," he continues, "You deserve this award because you're a one woman crime stopper, congratulations."

I feel great because I know he's right. The award will not only strengthen my position in the community, but it will also look very good on my record.

When I collect my mother to take her to the hospital she does nothing but moan for the entire journey. Everything connected with me is wrong it seems. The car is too high and it's ugly unlike her friend's car which is comfortable and beautiful. I'm dying to point out that her friend has not volunteered to drive her, but I bite my tongue. My clothes are too young and too bright, but of course my uniform would have been all wrong too. Apparently, my car also smells of dog, but then my mother doesn't smell too sweet either because she's rarely out of her black shift dress and I'm sure she only washes once a month. Then there's my use of makeup, which although is very light, makes me look like a whore, according to mother. It's clear, that whatever I say or do, I cannot get it right, so I drive in silence and count the minutes until we arrive at the hospital.

When we collect my father he's delighted to see me and he has a spring in his step that I'm sure is due to his new found job. It's clear he hasn't told my mother yet and he glances at me nervously as if warning me to say nothing. He has no fear of that happening, the pleasure of informing her will be all his. I drop them at the house and tell my father I'll telephone tomorrow to see how he is. He thanks me profusely for collecting him, but my mother does not, in fact she doesn't even say goodbye to me, but that's par for the course.

After lunch I decide to knock off early because I'm tired and I want to go home and tell Patricia about my award. It's then I realise I haven't told my parents or given them their invitations, but I don't want to go back to their house today, so it will have to keep.

CHAPTER 37

When I arrive home I hear voices coming from the kitchen and, as I enter, I see that Patricia is talking to Michel Albert. They're sitting at the table surrounded by pots of jams and pickles and when she sees me she comes over to talk to me.

"I hope you don't mind, Danielle," she says in a whisper, "But Michel's flight is not until seven o'clock so I brought him back here for some lunch. He's been sampling my jams and chutneys and I think he wants to order some for his restaurant."

Her face is so bright and happy that I decide to save my news for when we are alone.

"I hope I'm not intruding," Michel calls over. "Patricia has been very kind but I can get a cab now if my being here is inconvenient."

I'm aware that this man has just buried his mother and Patricia is enjoying his company.

"You're not intruding, Michel," I reply. "In fact, I'll drive you to Perpignan airport for your flight later. Please sit down and continue whatever you're doing while I go and get changed."

Patricia flashes me a beaming smile and mouths a kiss as Michel resumes sampling produce. I'm rather excited for Patricia because if Michel Albert does decide to use her produce, who knows where it might lead. I quickly get washed and changed then I make my way back downstairs and join them.

"How was the funeral?" I ask. "I take it that it passed without incident."

"It was very low key just as I wished it to be," Michel replies. "Although I was surprised at Mother's maid attending with her elderly aunt. She's a very strange little creature, but she insisted on showing her respects and, to be honest, I was quite touched she was there."

"I'm very surprised because she's been hiding from Raul and she was frightened of being seen. It's a measure of the high regard she had for your mother that she attended the funeral and exposed herself to risk."

We sit and chat some more, then Michel informs Patricia he'd like to order from her and she goes off to get her order book.

"You won't be disappointed," I say. "Patricia's jams and pickles are legendary."

When the order is written up the subject changes to the opening of Michel's new bistro in London, "You should both come to the grand opening," he says. "Only the rich and famous are invited to attend and it's likely to be the hottest ticket in town."

"Are you sure we'd fit the bill?" Patricia asks. "We are neither rich nor famous," she says winking at me. "We don't even own passports although we do have identity cards," she continues. "Neither of us has ever gone abroad apart from brief visits over the border to Spain."

"We've never been on a plane before," I add. "I wouldn't know how to go about booking one."

"Could you get the time off work?" Michel asks

"The grand opening is to be held a week on Saturday."

"I'm sure we could make the time if we flew over on the Friday night and came back on the Monday," I reply. "What do you think Patricia?"

"That shouldn't be a problem because Marjorie would look after Ollee for us, but we wouldn't know how to dress for such an occasion. And where would we stay in London?"

"I could help you book flights and a hotel tonight if you have the internet available here. While you're in London, I'll have a car chauffeur you around. It's the least I can do after the kindness you've both shown me. As for what to wear, it really doesn't matter because anything goes. There will be people wearing everything from formal wear to jeans."

Patricia and I hold our faces in our hands and look at each other, "Let's do it," she says. "If Michel can help us book the flights and the hotel then lets do it."

"You won't have to worry about a thing," Michel says and both he and Patricia are looking at me expectantly.

"When we get off the flight your driver will be waiting for us?" I ask. "So we won't get lost in London."

"I promise, absolutely, he will be there."

"Please say yes, Danielle, please, please." Patricia is hard to refuse.

"You better come over to the computer then, Michel," I say. "Because it looks as if we're going to London."

Patricia lets out a squeal of excitement and Ollee sits up and barks and we all laugh at him. I'm really scared, but sometimes it's good to do something that frightens you. Then you know you're living and not merely existing.

CHAPTER 38

By the time we drive Michel to the airport we're all booked up and raring to go. We've opted to fly from Girona in Spain instead of Perpignan because the flight will get us in at a better time. It will take us just over an hour to get to the Spanish airport instead of half an hour to the French one, but we'll be in central London by early afternoon instead of the evening.

"The hotel I've chosen for you is part of the Thistle group of hotels," Michel says. "It has four stars and, because of a special offer, I've managed to get you a free upgrade to an executive suite. Your room will be a 'no smoking room' so you won't have to endure the effects of someone else's dirty habit."

"I still don't quite understand how we have checked in both ways when we haven't even been to the airport," Patricia says from the back of the car.

I'm pleased she's mentioned this because I too didn't quite get it, but I didn't want to show my ignorance.

"It is sort of like travelling by bus Patricia," Michel explains. "The online check-in has told the company that you'll be travelling with one hold bag each, so now all you have to do when you arrive at the airport is hand your bag in at the drop off point and get on the plane. The boarding cards that I printed for you are your tickets so don't lose them. You will simply present them along with your identity cards."

"You make it all sound so simple," Patricia says but the hesitation in her voice lets me know she thinks it's anything but.

We have a few days until we are due to depart so I'll have time to familiarise myself with everything. I decide to drive to Girona airport before our travel date and find out exactly what the procedure is, that way I'll be confident when we actually travel.

"Don't worry, Darling, I'll keep us right," I say. "All you have to do is decide what to wear."

She's noticeably relieved by my confidence. "Don't worry about that, I'm going to buy a new outfit at the weekend and you can come and choose one too."

"Sounds good to me," I reply.

"Don't buy too much girls," Michel cuts in. "Remember you're going to London, land of the shopping. The reason I chose the Thistle Hotel for you is because it's at the corner of Oxford Street. You'll be in one of the best shopping areas in the world, so leave space in your cases for your purchases. Remember there are weight restrictions on the luggage."

"How will we know who our driver is when we arrive at the airport in London?" Patricia asks.

"He'll be holding a sign with your name on it," Michel replies. "Don't worry I won't let you get lost."

When we arrive at the airport in Perpignan I pull into the taxi drop off point and we say our goodbyes to Michel. I've enjoyed seeing him again, he's so unlike everything I expected. I thought he would be pompous and pretentious but he's nothing of the sort. On the drive home Patricia can talk of nothing except Michel this and London that so once again I save my news for later.

After we're home and seated at the table for dinner I finally get to tell Patricia about the 'Citizen of the Year' award.

"How marvellous for you," she says enthusiastically. "You deserve the recognition. You've worked so hard. We'll definitely have to go shopping at the weekend because we'll need new clothes for both the presentation and for London. I think we should go to Perpignan because none of our local shops are stylish enough and we could do with advice on what's appropriate. After we finish dinner I'll telephone Marjorie and make sure she can take Ollee when we're away, and I'll make arrangements for the cat and the chickens. We're turning into jetsetters and I'm really excited but a bit scared."

I feel exactly the same way and I'm pleased we are experiencing new things together because I probably wouldn't have done anything like this on my own.

"Do you think your mother and father will come to the presentation?" she asks. "It would be a real turnaround if your mother attends and is forced to support you by sitting in the front row. She'd have to admit that she's been wrong and has judged you unfairly. On the other hand, could she bear to stay away and miss the ceremony, when she has the chance to be seen by the whole town as the mother of the esteemed winner of the award?"

I think of my mother wearing her old black shift

dress and my father clothed in the one threadbare suit he owns and, I realise, this is one occasion I must try to build bridges. If they agree to attend the ceremony, I'll offer to take them to the outfitters in town and treat them to new clothes. If I tell them that I'm proud they're my parents, and without them I wouldn't be receiving the award, and the new outfits are my way of showing my appreciation, they might accept. It's not true of course, but I can't have them sitting in the front row looking like a pair of tramps.

CHAPTER 39

By Friday morning there's still no sign of Raymond Dupree, it's as if both he and Raul Armin have vanished off the face of the earth. I'm keeping Detective Gerard informed and, like me, he's more concerned about finding Raymond than Raul because Raymond is connected to us, so I decide to question his mother again just in case there is a relative or friend he could be staying with. When I get to the apartment block where they live I see that all the shutters are now open.

"Have you found him yet?" Madame Dupree asks as she opens the door.

"There's been no sign of him," I reply. "You must be very worried."

"If you must know, I've been much happier since he's been away. I felt so ashamed when he was living here, but now that he's gone I can go out of the house without being afraid of meeting people. Everyone is now sorry for me because my son is missing."

She is so matter of fact and unworried it's as if she's talking about a cat wandering off instead of her sick son. I can see I'm wasting my time here, as it's clear, she neither knows nor cares where he is.

"Is there any relative or friend he could be with," I venture.

"Everyone in the family has disowned him and,

it's obvious to me now, I never really knew my son, so I can't say if he has any friends."

"You do know he's mentally ill, Madame," I say, trying to stir some emotion in her. "He could be a danger to himself."

"If he is mad then the hospital should have kept him locked up and given him drugs. They had no right to send him back here. I hope the police department will ensure he doesn't step foot inside this house again."

I'm absolutely flabbergasted. This woman is so cold and heartless she could be my mother's clone. This meeting has been a complete waste of time and I feel very sad for Raymond. No wonder he's taken off, he must have felt so lonely when Veronique was murdered.

When I'm back in my office I have the overwhelming urge to speak to my Papa, so I risk my mother answering and I pick up the phone and dial their number. After three rings it's my father who picks up.

"Hello, Papa, how are you today?" I ask.

"Oh, it's you, Danielle," he replies. "I'm so pleased to hear from you. Your Mama and I are both well thank you. What's new?"

By the tone of his voice and what he's said, I can tell my mother is in the room. I speak to my father about Michel Albert and the forthcoming trip to London. He's very interested that all the arrangements have been made using the internet. Then I pluck up the courage to tell him about the presentation I am to receive. He's thrilled and he tells me how proud he is of me, then assures me that both he and my mother will attend the ceremony.

"Just you try and stop us," he says. "Your mother and I will be in the front row to see our wonderful daughter receive the recognition she deserves, won't we Mama?"

Once again I'm aware he's including my mother in the conversation. I obviously don't know if she's happy about attending or not, but he's leaving her little choice in the matter.

"I'm so pleased you're coming," I say truthfully. "I'd like to show my appreciation for all your support by buying you and Mama new outfits to wear on the day. Will you allow me to do that for you?"

"How kind of you Danielle, your mother and I will accept your kind gift, but the truth is, you achieved this honour on your own, we had nothing to do with it."

Everything he says is true and in fact rather than encourage me, my mother tried, at every opportunity, to put obstacles in my way. However, this is not the time for recriminations. I arrange with Papa that he and Mama will buy their new clothes from a local outfitters and I will pay the bill. The clothes will not be very stylish, but at least they'll be new and no better or worse than the clothes worn by anyone else in town.

I feel so happy to be talking to my father in this way. To be able to pick up the phone and call him and have a normal conversation with him, without my mother adding her venom, is a new experience for me. In the past she would always take control and come between us, and he always took her side for fear of upsetting her, but perhaps this is a turning point for us all.

CHAPTER 40

The sun is shining through a crack in the curtains and no matter which way I turn it shines in my eyes. I look at the clock beside my bed and see it's seven o'clock. As it's Saturday, and I have the day off, I don't have to get up this early, but the morning brightness is relentless. I'm not actually tired I simply don't want to move.

Patricia and I are going to Perpignan this morning so we can buy our new clothes. I suppose, if she also wakes early, we can get there in time for the shops opening and maybe it will be quieter and easier to shop. Saturday is always hectic in the centre of Perpignan and the tourist season is not yet over.

I get up, wash and dress, and I hope the sounds of me moving about the house will wake Patricia. It's a bit unkind of me to want her to get up early just because I'm awake, but she won't complain about it when we're shopping ahead of the crowds. With a bit more banging around, I get my wish, and by eight-thirty we are on our way.

As I approach the centre of Perpignan I'm surprised by the amount of traffic on the roads. Normally I would try to park on or near Boulevard Wilson but the streets are packed. After driving around for a few minutes I spot a poster advertising the 'Marche Medieval' and I realise why the place is so busy. This annual event is held in 'Campo Santo' which is the only cloistered cemetery in France. It's a vast open square surrounded by the cloisters. It's often used for exhibitions and markets.

"Merde," I say. "I should have remembered this was on. At least, if we do get parked, the shops should be quiet, because everyone will be at the Medieval Market."

Suddenly, I see that a car is pulling out of a really superb space right in front of me and I'm in the perfect position to pull straight in to it. It's a real stroke of luck.

"Maybe after we shop we could visit the market," Patricia says. "It would be nice to take some time out and do something different."

Now I've parked the car I have no problem with that and, I agree with her, it might be good fun, but for the time being the shops are beckoning. We enter one of the bigger department stores, but we're at a bit of a loss as neither one of us has much shopping experience. A young sales assistant asks us if we need help and we tell her we do and, because the store is quiet, she becomes our personal shopper. Within an hour, both Patricia and I have two new outfits each, and our young helper also picks out appropriate accessories for us. As everything is rung up at the till I see we've spent just under six hundred euros, but instead of being shocked by the amount, I'm simply delighted with our purchases. What a difference the lottery win has made, I think.

We leave the store with a spring in our step and go back to the car to dump the shopping then we make our way to Campo Santo. As we near the place, we see people of all shapes and sizes dressed in Medieval costumes and, as we enter the square, we are faced with amazing sights.

There are fire eaters, sword fights and the 'Chevaliers Du Roussillon', are putting on a show of dagger combats. There are street theatre shows with lepers and thieves and public executions. Surrounding all of this, there are demonstrations, stalls selling honey, cheese, wine and cakes and there is free sampling of everything.

Patricia is particularly interested in the demonstrations of lace making and jewellery making and I'm fascinated by the iron worker. We walk about for over two hours and we're just about fit to drop, so we make our way to one of the food stalls and sit down to eat. The food is delicious. I wolf down a stew of pork and beans washed down by beer then I tuck into a huge piece of moist, aromatic, lemon sponge cake. I finish my meal with rich, black coffee, but that's not enough to keep me from wanting to put my head down and sleep. The amount of time on my feet, plus the rich food and early start, has made it difficult for me to stay awake and I find myself drifting off in my chair. I wake with a start at the sound of the cathedral bells ringing out and, when I look at my watch, I realise that I must have dozed for about twenty minutes.

"Oh, you're back," Patricia says laughing. "You were completely out of it there and snoring like Ollee, but I didn't have the heart to wake you."

"I don't snore," I say indignantly, but in truth, I

know that I do. Sometimes I even wake myself with snoring.

She looks at me and pulls a face then she pretends to snore and I find myself laughing.

"You'd better shut up or I'll let you walk home."

We have one more tour of the market and buy some wine and cheese then we return to the car. It's been wonderful not to have to think about the cost before we purchase things and I'm delighted that this will now be our way of life.

CHAPTER 41

The phone rings at nine o'clock on Sunday morning and I wonder who would telephone at this hour. Patricia is feeding the chickens so I answer it.

"Hello, Danielle, I hope I didn't wake you." It's my Papa and I immediately get a jag of fear because he's always rung my mobile in the past, never the house phone.

"Are you okay, Papa, is anything wrong?"

"Everything is good, Danielle," he says and I'm reassured. "I just wondered if I could come and visit you because I'd like to see your house. Your Mama is at church. Afterwards, she's going to her friend to have lunch and to plan the Autumn Festival, so I'll be on my own."

I'm thrilled, because neither my mother nor my Papa has ever set foot in this house before and we've lived here for over two years.

"Will you have lunch with Patricia and me?" I ask. "We'd love you to stay. Perhaps afterwards I can drive us to the orchard for a look around."

"That would be great, Danielle. It'll give me a chance to make plans with Patricia and I'd love to spend some time with you."

"I'll come right now and pick you up, Papa. I'll just tell Patricia I am leaving, she's feeding the chickens. Expect me in about fifteen minutes."
"Would you rather I walked? It would save you the

drive," he offers.

I'm touched he would even consider walking when he's just out of hospital.

"I wouldn't hear of it, Papa. You just get ready and wait for me, I won't be long."

We say our goodbyes and I run outside to tell Patricia.

"I'm so happy he's coming," she says. "We'll have a wonderful lunch in the garden and we'll be able to visit our orchard. I'll tidy up the house while you go and fetch him. He'll be so impressed with this house and what you've achieved."

"What we've achieved," I correct.

"I have one admission to make, Danielle," she adds. "I'm ashamed to say that I'm very pleased your mother isn't coming because I find her very difficult company."

"At least she's not related to you," I reply. "I'm stuck with her whether I like it or not."

As I leave Ollee comes running after me so I open the car door and let him accompany me. Just as I reach my father's house, my mobile phone rings and I answer it without looking at the number because I assume it's a call from Patricia. I'm surprised to hear a strange woman's voice ask for me.

"It's me, Phoebe," the voice says. "Do you remember me? You gave me your number. I used to work for Madame Henriette."

I remember her. She was one of Madame's girls. "What do you want at this time on a Sunday morning?" I ask. "I'm not working just now. It's my day off".

"I'm sorry, but I didn't know what else to do. I couldn't phone the police station because it concerns a policeman."

As soon as she says that I know Raymond must have paid her a visit. "Where are you?" I ask.

"After my apartment was trashed I stayed with a friend in Elne. I thought I was safe because only the police knew my address. Then officer Dupree turned up at the door and I got scared and I moved to Argeles. Please come, I must talk to you. I'm very frightened."

I ask her for the address and assure her I'm the only person who'll know it then I tell her I'll call on her later today. I'm angry, that once again, I've discovered Raymond has been given confidential information while on suspension, but I put all thoughts of him from my mind as Ollee and I go to collect my father.

CHAPTER 42

When I arrive at my father's house he's waiting on the doorstep for me. He's holding a bunch of flowers.

"I hope you like these," he says. "Your mother never liked having cut flowers in the house. My neighbour grows these roses and, when I told him I was visiting with my daughter the cop, he cut these for me. He mentioned you helped him when his car broke down and he says that he's going to the award ceremony to applaud you."

My father has a look of unashamed pride on his face and I'm rather embarrassed by this, even though I know I deserve the accolade. As we head off Ollee tries to climb into the front seat and onto my father's knee. I'm shouting at the stupid dog to move and my father is helpless with laughter. It's a sound I don't remember hearing for a very long time.

"Where did you get this comedian?" he asks.

"Patricia rescued him when an old man collapsed in the street. She later found out that the dog wasn't his and we were stuck with him. He's the centre of her universe now. He gets better treatment than me."

"Are you and Patricia a couple, Danielle?" my father asks. I know it's a very difficult question for him and he's probably afraid of the answer.

"We are not lovers, Papa, just loving friends," I reply.

"I see, I see," he replies and I can tell he's relieved. "I hope I didn't embarrass you by asking. Your reply makes no difference to me, you're my daughter and I love you, no matter what, but I just wanted to know."

"I understand Papa and I don't suppose anything I tell you will make a difference to Mama."

"Your Mama must live with her own demons and nothing you say or do will change that. None of it is your fault, Danielle. She had strange ideas even before you were born."

I wish I'd known this information years ago because it might have made my childhood easier to bear. I always blamed myself for my mother's problems.

Patricia is waiting outside the house when we arrive and, as he steps out of the car, she greets my father with a hug and a kiss.

"What a lovely home you have," he says as we show him around. "It's much bigger inside than it looks from the outside and it's in lovely condition."

We go through the house to the back garden and I sit my father down in my favourite chair. Patricia brings out coffee and sponge cake.

"This is an idyllic setting, girls," he says. "You have the garden set out beautifully."

"Wait till you see the walled garden across the road," Patricia replies. "We have our henhouse and our rabbit hutches there. In fact, we'll be using our own eggs and vegetables for lunch."

"Patricia is a wonderful cook," I tell my father.

"Her produce is sold all over the region and she's now going to be supplying a celebrity chef in Paris with her pickles."

"So you're both successful, well done," he replies.

We spend a very pleasant morning chatting like a normal family and I'm so happy this meeting is taking place. After lunch I drive my father and Patricia to the orchard and, after careful inspection, we return to the house so they can discuss their future plans. It's mid-afternoon before I take my father back to his house and I can see that he's beginning to tire.

"I hope you haven't overdone things, Papa," I say and I'm genuinely concerned.

"I am perfectly fine, Danielle," he answers. "I'm old enough and wise enough to know that I must take an afternoon nap each day until I regain my strength. I'll go and lie down as soon as I get inside. I've had a lovely time with you and Patricia and I hope it's the start of things to come. We've all wasted too much time pussyfooting around your mother but that will change now."

"I love you, Papa," I say and I throw my arms around his neck and kiss him. As I hug him, I can see my mother is home because I catch a glimpse of her at the kitchen window, but she doesn't acknowledge me and instead draws back from my view.

"I love you too, Danielle," he replies.

When he leaves the car I drive home to change into my uniform before going to Argeles to call on Phoebe. It's another annoyance and I would much rather spend the rest of my day with Patricia, but I'm so happy I've had time with my darling Papa that nothing can change my good mood.

CHAPTER 43

As the name suggests Argeles-sur-Mer is a seaside town and it's very popular with tourists. During July and August the population of ten thousand swells by ten times with many of the visitors staying in the numerous surrounding campsites. The old town of Argeles is actually about one kilometre inland and if you want the beach area you must make your way to Argeles Plage on the Cote Vermeille.

It is a town of contrasts with the old town having narrow cobbled streets and the seafront area having more modern developments. The beach is a seven kilometre stretch of fine golden sand. It has stunning natural beauty and is enhanced by the hills of Les Alberes which rise up behind it.

At this time of year Argeles Plage is much quieter because the school holidays have just finished. Only a few older tourists who can take their holidays at any time of the year remain, and it never ceases to amaze me that one day you can hardly move along the pavement which flanks the beach, and the next day is so quiet you can roller skate along it.

The address that Phoebe has given me is for a large house which is situated immediately behind the seafront. Only a neat grassy area separates this house from the beach. When I ring the bell the door is opened by the biggest man I've ever seen. He is easily six and a half feet tall and he has the physique of a body builder. The doorway is filled with his massive frame. He is dressed in a sleeveless top and shorts and his thighs are about the size of my waist, his head is completely bald and his suntanned skin glistens with a mixture of sweat and oil. I cannot take my eyes off this giant of a man, it's impossible not to stare at him.

"What do you want," he says and, even though I'm in uniform, I feel myself shrink under his gaze.

"I am here to see Phoebe," I reply. "I do have the correct address don't I?"

I know I have the right address, but I don't want a confrontation with this giant, who would?

"You'd better come in," he says and he steps aside to let me enter. He shows me into the lounge which is situated at the front of the house. It is a large, bright room furnished with expensive modern furniture. The picture windows offer magnificent sea views. Phoebe is stretched out on a modern chaise longue and, when I enter the room, she turns to me. She doesn't get up, but she points to a comfortable armchair opposite her.

"Please sit down, Officer," she says. "Thank you for coming."

I get straight to the point, "You say you've been contacted by Officer Dupree, do you want to tell me about it?"

"I was staying with my friend in Elne because I was hiding from Raul, as you know," she begins, "When the doorbell went at ten o'clock one night I thought it was my friend returning because she'd forgotten her keys, but when I answered the door it was

Officer Dupree who was standing there. I told him I had nothing to say to him and I tried to close the door, but he forced his way into the house. I was very frightened, he was acting very strangely and he kept muttering to himself and arguing with himself."

"Did he say why he was there or what he wanted from you?" I ask.

"He was trying to find Raul and, when I said that I didn't know where he was, Officer Dupree became agitated and his manner was very aggressive. I'm just lucky that Robert here turned up because I don't know what would have happened if he hadn't. Robert is the cousin of my friend Chloe who I'd been staying with."

"I had to physically take the policeman out of the house because he refused to leave," Robert says. "He was very agitated and he was making threats, which is why Phoebe is now staying here. The police need to rein in this officer because he's a real nut job."

It's clear by his accent Robert is English and, it's clear by the quality of this house, he has a lot of money.

"So neither of you gave any indication to Officer Dupree of where Raul Armin might be," I say.

"Phoebe told him nothing," Robert says, "But I suggested to him he should perhaps look for Raul in the town of Le Perthus."

"What made you think he might be there?" I ask.

"As you no doubt realise I'm a body builder," Robert says. "I own a gym in Perpignan where rich, young professionals go to train. Many of these people buy supplements to help them build their bodies but sometimes the supplements are in short supply here. Raul has a contact in Spain and he would often go and pick up stock in Le Perthus because it's a frontier town."

"Are these supplements steroids?" I ask.

"I wouldn't sell illegal drugs, Officer," he says with a wry smile and I know that I have hit the nail on the head, no wonder he has so much money.

We talk for a few minutes more and I give Robert my card. I ask him to get in touch if he thinks of anything else that might help my investigation, but I won't hold my breath. Now that Phoebe has said her piece I don't think I'll hear from either of them again.

I'm concerned that we can't locate Raymond. He seems relentless in his pursuit of Raul. We must find him before he gets hurt. Two dead whores I can deal with because no one really cares about them, but if Raymond comes to harm, it's a different story.

CHAPTER 44

On Sunday evening I receive a call from Marjorie to ask if my mother and Papa will be attending the award ceremony and I confirm that they will. I tell her I want to buy them new outfits for the occasion, but I'm so busy, I just don't know when I can arrange the time for the shopping trip. She finds it amusing when I tell her that Patricia has refused to accompany them on my behalf, but when I explain to her the way my mother talks to Patricia, she can fully understand why.

"Don't stress, Danielle," Marjorie says, "I'll take them. You tell me what you want to spend and we can settle up later."

"My mother can be extremely difficult," I warn, "Are you sure you want to do this?"

"Don't worry about a thing, Danielle. I can be just as difficult when I'm pushed too far. Besides, she can hardly misbehave when she's in the company of the Mayor's wife. They'll both look great when I've finished with them, which is just as well, because you'll be expected to have your photo taken with your proud Mama and Papa for the local newspaper. I'm so pleased to be able to do something for you after the way you helped me over the Madame Henriette business."

I accept her kind offer and it takes such a weight off my mind because I was dreading shopping with my mother. I know Marjorie will do a good job because she has impeccable taste.

As I expected the next couple of days disappear under a mountain of paperwork, suddenly it's Wednesday, and the day of the ceremony. Marjorie telephones me and tells me my mother behaved very well during the shopping trip. She's offered to collect my parents and take them to the town hall for the event and they've accepted. I cannot thank her enough because I'm already nervous about being given the honour, without the added pressure of dealing with my mother's potentially difficult behaviour. It was such a good idea for Patricia and me to buy new outfits to wear for this occasion, because it's another thing I don't have to worry about. We are dressed and ready to step out of the door in good time when my mobile rings and, when I look at the screen, I see that it's Detective Gerard calling. I almost don't answer it because I fear he's going to pull me up for not yet catching up with Raul Armin, and for losing Raymond Dupree, but my fears are unfounded.

"I'm glad I caught you," he says when I answer. "I wanted to congratulate you on the honour you're about to receive. I've sent a journalist from Perpignan along with a photographer, so we can write a feature about you for the police magazine. It's not every day that an officer is honoured in this way and we must make the most of it."

I'm stunned and delighted by what he's said. "Thank you, Sir," I say. "I am truly honoured, you are very kind."

"Not at all, not at all. The best support we can

get is the backing of the general public, because they have the means to make or break us. You are obviously getting the balance between police work and social acceptance just right to win this award. I'm recommending you for a commendation for your excellent work in the community. Well done, Danielle."

When he hangs up I tell Patricia what he's said.

"It just keeps getting better and better, doesn't it?" she says and I have to admit, it does.

When we arrive at the town hall the place is packed and, as I make my way to the stage, I can see my mother and Papa sitting in the front row beside Marjorie. She has reserved the seat beside her for Patricia. I'm amazed at the transformation of my parents. Who could have imagined that a new suit of clothes could change their looks so much?

My mother is wearing a lovely tailored dress in a soft shade of lilac and over it, she has a smart navy blue jacket with a Chanel collar. Her shoes and bag are a matching shade of navy, and her hair has been coloured and cut in a style that frames her face and shows off her small features. My father is in a well-tailored, dark blue suit with a crisp white shirt and Paisley print tie. His shoes have been polished to a mirror finish. His face is freshly shaven and his hair is stylishly cut. They look like a million dollars. They don't look like my parents.

Marjorie sees me staring and she comes over to talk to me, "Well?" she asks, "What do you think?"

I don't know what to say, seeing my parents

looking so good and so much younger than they did before, overwhelms me. Tears of emotion threaten to run down my cheeks.

"Hey, hey, don't do that or your mascara will run. You don't want to look like a giant panda in the photos," Marjorie says. "A simple thank you will be enough. I don't require tears. By the way, that transformation has cost you a fortune, so you might well cry."

I'm so overcome I can't find the words to tell her how grateful I am, so I just nod my head and smile. She walks with me to where my parents are seated and I thank them for coming and tell them how wonderful they look. My Papa is beaming proudly at me and even my mother manages a smile.

When I look up at the stage I can see there are a number of awards laid out on a table, so I'm not the only person who'll be honoured tonight. I'm about to climb the stairs to take my place on the stage when the journalist from Perpignan comes over to take my picture. He assembles me with my mother and Papa but doesn't include Patricia in the shot as he thinks it would be inappropriate. I feel quite upset by this, but Patricia says to let it go. However, she does get him to take a photograph of the two of us together and he promises to send us a copy.

All the presentations and speeches are over in less than three hours, but I'm so exhausted by the proceedings, I'm worried that if we hang around talking much longer, I might fall asleep while driving us home. So we say our goodbyes and leave as early as we can without offending anyone. Once again Marjorie comes to my rescue by offering to drive my parents home.

When at last we reach our house and I park the car, I'm relieved to be able to kick off my shoes and relax.

"One down, one to go," I say. "On Friday we'll embark on another adventure when we fly to London, but in the meantime, I feel as if I could sleep for a week."

"Me too," Patricia says. "Being a celebrity is very, very tiring."

I have to agree with her but I must admit that it's also very exciting and my heart is racing just thinking about our trip.

CHAPTER 45

I'm still tired on Thursday morning and there's so much to do. Because I'll be out of the office Friday to Monday with the London trip, I must organise the work so Paul and Laurent can cope in my absence. There are just not enough hours in the day because every nutcase and time waster in town has chosen this morning to walk through the door and ask stupid questions.

At least I'm now fairly confident about the procedure at Girona airport, for both parking the car and dropping off the luggage, and Michel has told us what to do in order to pass through security and board the plane. By the time I get home today Patricia will have our cases packed and all our documents will be in her handbag. It seems I'm not to be trusted with these vital pieces of paper. On the odd free moments in between dealing with the public or answering the phone, I get a jag of excitement whenever I think about the trip.

Usually my day passes fairly slowly, but today the hours rush by like an express train. I find myself driving home, with everything that's happened between waking and now, a blur. As I step through the front door, the house is unusually quiet and I realise it's because Marjorie has already collected Ollee for his little holiday. It's amazing how much presence one little dog can have. The house feels strange without his greeting and slobbery kisses. Patricia is pacing the floor anxiously with a check list in her hand.

"What if we forget something?" she asks nervously. "What will we do?"

"London is not a third world country," I reply. "If we forget something we'll simply buy it there. Please stop panicking or you'll get me started. The only things we really have to have are the three cards, our boarding cards, our identity cards and a credit card, the hotel voucher and our cases are both important but replaceable."

"I hope that Michel's driver turns up for us," she says, stressing further.

"If he doesn't we'll simply get a taxi. Don't worry we will be fine."

"How are you so calm when I'm all over the place?" she asks.

"I'm used to handling all different experiences with my job, so new challenges don't get to me," I reply. I'm lying of course. I'm simply trying to calm her down because she's making me even more nervous than I already am.

After dinner I telephone my Papa to see how he is and he sounds really well and happy. I ask after my mother and I'm very surprised when she takes the phone from him so she can wish me a good trip. She makes no mention of Patricia but her enquiring about me is a new experience. Little by little, I think.

I receive a call from the emergency switchboard to inform me there's a fire at a disused farm house and they ask me if I'll be attending, but for the first time in a long time, I decline. The switchboard operator assures me that no-one is in danger and the building is abandoned. Usually, I try to attend every incident when there's a fire, but in this instance, I refer them to Paul, because I'm on holiday.

      Patricia and I manage, with difficulty, to eat our dinner, but the excitement of the forthcoming trip has robbed us of our appetite. Our flight is not until lunchtime tomorrow and it's just as well, because neither of us is sleepy and the hours are ticking away. We try watching television and reading, we even have hot milky drinks, but sleep evades us. It's after one a.m. and we're still sitting downstairs talking. Eventually, we decide we must at least try to rest so we head upstairs to our bedrooms. I'm very tired even though my brain is fighting sleep and, when I do lie down, I feel myself begin to relax. I must have fallen asleep quite quickly after that because when I wake in the morning I notice my bedside lamp is still switched on. I lie in bed for a few minutes and go through a checklist in my head of things to remember before we set off on holiday. Today's the day, I think, and I'm tingling with excitement. No turning back now, London here we come.

CHAPTER 46

As we near Gerona airport my hands are shaking holding the steering wheel. I'm trying to give the impression that I'm in control for Patricia's sake, but in truth, I'm quaking. I hadn't actually thought about the flying part of the trip, now the prospect of being in a metal tube travelling at a very high speed in order to avoid crashing into the ground, terrifies me. I try to push the thought from my mind and concentrate on negotiating the airport signs. We manage to find the car park and we leave the car then wheel our suitcases into the terminal. It's familiar to me because I've already had a dry run. After we drop off our hold luggage we pass through security without a hitch, because I was prepared for not being allowed to carry things, like nail files, manicure scissors or face cream in our hand luggage.

We have two hours to kill before our flight so we spend the time having coffee and a snack and scouring the shops. The one thing we each have forgotten is to pack a book to read, but that's quickly remedied at the newsagent's stand. Half an hour before our flight is due, I find myself constantly looking at the screen which shows today's departures, and I get a surge of excitement when our Stansted flight changes from 'wait in lounge' to 'go to gate'. Just as Michel instructed, we show our identity cards and boarding cards, then we're passed through to walk to the plane.

"Where do we sit?" Patricia asks me. "Which seat number is ours?"

"Sit anywhere," I reply. "It is free seating so just sit anywhere you like."

Once again having prior knowledge is very reassuring. We watch the stewardess intently as she runs through the safety procedure and my hands start to shake, so I grip the armrests and pray silently to myself. Dear God, please don't let us crash, I think, but if we do and people must die, let it not be us. Selfish I know, but what the hell, being selfish is acceptable in my book if your life is at stake. When the plane does finally finish its journey down the runway and successfully takes off, I breathe a sigh of relief. The flight time passes quickly because we are distracted by the stewardesses coming round to offer food and drinks and various items to buy and, before very long, we're on the ground and heading for the baggage reclaim. We're relieved to see our cases appear and we collect them, then pass straight out of the customs 'European Union Arrivals' doorway and into the airport. Within a couple of minutes of scouring the waiting people, I see a man in a chauffeur's uniform holding a card with Patricia's name on it, and we make our way to him. He immediately introduces himself as Thomas. He takes our cases and asks us to please follow him, which we do. I don't know what I expected, but it certainly wasn't the beautiful wine coloured Bentley. We sink into the sumptuous leather seats and we just can't stop grinning.

"There's champagne or whisky in the bar."

Thomas says, "Please, help your selves, ladies".

I can't believe it, a bar in a car whatever next. The champagne is in half size bottles so we plump for that and we're soon sipping away at it and munching on peanuts. Almost immediately, we pass housing estates and I think we'll soon be at our hotel, but I'm mistaken because I'd no idea just how big London is. It's a long journey before we arrive in Central London and I'm overwhelmed by the sheer scale of it. When we pull up outside the hotel, I'm surprised to discover that the main entrance is in quite a narrow back street.

"The front of the hotel overlooks Oxford Street so you couldn't be in a better position for shopping, ladies," Thomas says as he helps us from the car.

He hands our cases to the concierge and gives me a card with his telephone number written on it.

"When you require the car just call this number about half an hour beforehand and I'll come and fetch you. I'll collect you tonight at five-thirty to drive you for a pre-theatre meal then I'll take you to the theatre for a show. Mister Albert has taken the liberty of arranging this for you and he hopes it's acceptable. He's sorry he can't join you tonight, but he's busy with the arrangements for the opening of the restaurant." Thomas hands us an envelope. "Here are your tickets and a programme for the show."

We hadn't expected Michel to do any more for us because he's already done so much, but the prospect of dinner then a show is fantastic. I thank Thomas sincerely for his kind attention. I'm not sure whether or not he expects a tip, but I don't offer one for fear of offending him, then we make our way to an escalator that carries us up to the hotel reception. It takes no time to check in then we take the lift to the sixth floor and our executive suite. When we enter the room we're delighted by everything we see. I've never stayed in a four star hotel before and this one lives up to all my expectations. Patricia and I are thrilled. We throw ourselves down on the well-sprung mattresses of the twin beds and giggle like teenage girls.

CHAPTER 47

We unpack our cases and hang our clothes in the wardrobe. It takes us only a few minutes because we've brought very little with us. Patricia discovers a refrigerator in a cupboard under the television and, on the top of it, there's a tray with a kettle and lots of little sachets containing tea, coffee, chocolate drink, sugar, milk and even biscuits. We're not very sure if we'll be charged for using these items, but we cannot resist making a cup of chocolate each and munching on shortbread biscuits. As we sit sipping our hot chocolates I open the envelope with the theatre tickets and programme. The show is called 'Le Cage au Folles' and I think it's been chosen for us because it's in French. However, when I read the programme I see that it's not in French after all, but in English, and it's a comedy about a high class gay nightclub and the gay couple who own it.

"Perhaps it was chosen for us because it's gay," Patricia says.

"Speak for yourself," I reply and we laugh.

"My English is not as good as yours you might have to interpret for me," she says.

I don't think it will need much interpretation. From the programme it seems to be mostly singing and dancing."

"It was so kind of Michel to do this for us, it must have cost a lot of money. I thought we were rich with the lottery win, but when I saw the car and chauffeur, I realised that our comprehension of rich is on a different scale to Michel's."

There's a little spare time before we have to get ready for our meal and the theatre, so we decide to venture out onto Oxford Street. The short walk from the doorway of our hotel is relatively quiet, but when we reach Oxford Street we're shocked by the myriad of people rushing about and the cacophony of sound. Patricia grabs my arm to steady herself against the bustling crowd and we stand like a lone tree being battered by a storm.

"Where shall we go?" she shouts in my ear.

I look around to try to get my bearings because I am frightened to wander off into the crowd and get lost. We are on the corner of the street. A shop called 'Next' is beside us. Across the busy road is another shop called 'Primark', so if we do wander off, I have landmarks for finding my way back.

"Let's go into this shop," Patricia says answering her own question. "I like the look of the clothes in the window and the prices are quite cheap compared to Perpignan."

We enter 'Next' and we're relieved when it's quieter inside than on the street. Within an hour we've managed to buy several items of clothing and we are exhausted, so we return to our hotel. Our first shopping trip into the streets of London has got us no further than the shop on the corner, but it has been successful. When we enter the hotel my ears are still ringing from the noise outside and I wonder how people can spend their whole lives in such a place and at such a pace.

Once back in our room I place my purchases on the floor and I lay down on my bed. Patricia is going to have her shower before I have mine and she comes out of the bathroom to show me all the little bottles of shampoo and shower gel that have been left for us, then she disappears back into the bathroom and I hear the shower running. The next thing I know I'm being woken up.

"Come on sleepy head," Patricia says. "It's your turn to get washed".

I don't remember nodding off, and I hope the shower will wake me up, because I'm groggy after my unplanned sleep. I'm excited to be here in London, because before coming here, I couldn't have imagined what this city was like, but the small town girl in me craves the safety, peace and quiet of home. I feel completely out of my depth here and, once this experience is over, I'll be perfectly happy if I never set foot in London again.

At the pre-arranged time we meet Thomas in the lobby of our hotel and he whisks us off to the restaurant for our meal. He indicates the street we should walk down to reach the theatre once we have finished eating then he shows us where he'll be waiting for us after the show ends. I have no idea where I am or how I'd get back to the hotel under my own steam, but at least I've had the good sense to take the name and address of the hotel with me. Having it makes me feel safer because, if for any reason Thomas doesn't come back for us, I could at least try to get us a taxi.

We successfully negotiate our way to the theatre after our meal. The show is a gay romp based on a very lightweight story. However, the dancing is superb and Patricia loves every aspect of the experience. I'm delighted to see our car waiting outside when we exit the theatre because now I can relax. Thomas holds open the passenger door for us and we climb inside and, as he closes the door behind us, people clamour round and peer through the car windows.

"They think you're celebrities because you have a chauffeur driven Bently waiting for you," he explains.

It's a very claustrophobic experience.

"Tomorrow night will be worse because the paparazzi will be at the restaurant, but don't let them upset you." We glance around nervously as people bump against the car. "Just pretend they're not there," he continues.

I know his advice is probably sound, but it's impossible to follow. I feel like a goldfish in a bowl.

From the minute we wake on Saturday morning, until Thomas picks us up for the restaurant opening, the day passes in a blur, of shopping, resting and eating. We make it a bit further along Oxford Street this time, but that's as far as we get. The hotel is now beginning to feel more familiar and several times during the day we escape from the busy street to the safety of our room. When we are dressed and in the car on our way to the grand opening of the restaurant, I'm quite apprehensive about the greeting we'll get from the press. I steel myself ready for the experience, but nothing prepares me for the onslaught that awaits us.

Amidst cries of, 'look this way' and 'what's your name, pet?' Patricia and I run the gauntlet of flashing lights and microphones and it's a relief when we finally make it to the front door, show our invitations to the security men, and enter the restaurant.

Michel pops over to greet us, but we see very little of him during the rest of the evening because he's so busy meeting and greeting the rich and famous. Patricia is in her element and she's constantly pointing out to me people she recognises from the television or from magazines. After a half an hour of mingling with this crowd, I've had enough. The people here are not interested in anything other than promoting themselves. They seem shallow and I'll be delighted to leave their company.

After what seems forever the evening finally begins to wind down. Patricia and I say our goodbyes and once again we negotiate the press who are waiting like a pack of wild dogs at the door. When we throw ourselves into the car I exhale my bated breath with relief and Patricia bursts into giggles with the excitement of it all. It's clear that we've each had very different experiences. I'll be happy when our trip is over and we can return to our calm life in France. Patricia, on the other hand, is just getting into the swing of things here.

Sunday arrives and we have arranged that Thomas will pick us up and drive us round the sights of London. I'm much happier about this planned day because we can enjoy ourselves, but be out of the limelight. He's going to take us to Buckingham Palace and Trafalgar Square, and also to places that Patricia has seen in films, such as Notting Hill and Covent Garden. I've brought my camera and Thomas very kindly takes our photographs in front of every monument. I'm pleased that we'll have photos of this experience because I won't be rushing back here any time soon. By five o'clock we're exhausted and Thomas heads back towards the hotel. As we near our destination the car phone rings, it is Michel asking if we'll join him for dinner, and, as it will be the perfect ending to our holiday, we're delighted to accept his kind invitation.

CHAPTER 48

We have dinner at Michel's new restaurant. It looks much different without the noise and bustle of the previous evening and I really enjoy the superb meal in the beautiful surroundings. The restaurant is busy, in fact Michel tells us it is fully booked for the next six weeks, but he's kept this table free for our use. I am flattered, particularly when I see the menu and realise it would have cost us at least sixty pounds each to eat here and that's without the wine.

When we are near the end of our meal, a short, red-haired woman dressed all in black approaches our table. She is rail thin and she carries a gold coloured handbag that is almost the same size as her. She introduces herself as Mollie Kendal and explains she is a freelance journalist and she'd like to write an article about Patricia. It seems Michel has spoken to her and he mentioned that Patricia has started her own business, producing pickles and jams in the Pyrenees Oriental area of France. He also told Mollie about her painting and the success she's found as an artist.

Mollie says that Patricia's quick rise from being an assistant at a funeral parlour, to where she is now, is a real human interest story and her readers would like to hear about it. She's very enthusiastic and says that the area where we live is considered to be very romantic and in vogue at the moment. She's pushing Patricia to agree and her attitude irritates me.

Patricia is shy and unsure. I don't want her to be bullied into anything by this woman so I step in and say, "It's very kind of you to come over and introduce yourself Mollie. Do leave your card and Patricia will consider your offer. In the meantime, please excuse us as this is our last evening in London and we have much that we wish to discuss with Michel."

She stands and blinks her eyes at us for a moment and I can tell that she's unused to being dismissed and she's annoyed with me, but I don't care. She looks pleadingly at Michel and I get the impression she was hoping to be invited to join us, but he just shrugs and says nothing. With a big sigh, she reaches into her handbag and takes out her business card which she hands to Patricia, then she makes a show of kissing Michel, offers her hand to Patricia to shake, then says goodbye and leaves. The pushy cow didn't shake hands with me I note, but I don't care because my only interest is Patricia.

The rest of the evening passes without incident and, before very long, we're back in the Bentley travelling to our hotel. When we arrive we make for our suite and pack our bags. The nearly empty suitcases that we brought with us are now full of our purchases. All that remains is for us to get a good night's sleep, eat breakfast then return to the airport for our flight home.

We've packed a lot into a short trip and I'll be glad to leave London. It definitely wouldn't be my choice of a place to live as everyone is always in a hurry and nobody has time to stop and talk. As a foreign visitor I find the city very unfriendly and the people cold and distant. I know there were occasions that Patricia found it all rather glamorous, but the cost of that glamour is just too great in terms of what you must sacrifice.

On Monday morning when we are, at last, at the airport I hand Thomas a box of Belgian chocolates I've bought for him. I was unsure about tipping, but he seems pleased with my gift, so I hope I've done the right thing. We wave to him as he drives off, but he doesn't respond. I don't think he sees us because he's concentrating on the very busy road. I don't know how anyone can drive here safely, because I've never seen so many cars being driven by so many bad drivers.

When we enter the airport we manage to find a sign that directs us to the correct place to drop off our bags then we pass through security. Our flight is due to depart in under two hours and I'm pleased that we'll soon be on the plane and heading for home. Patricia is very quiet and I ask her if there is anything wrong.

"Do I have to talk to Mollie Kendal?" she asks, "I really don't want to be in a magazine and I don't want anyone knowing my life story."

"Show me her card," I say and she obediently reaches into her purse for it and hands it to me. I rip the card into little pieces and drop the pieces into a bin. "You never have to think about her again," I say and I'm relieved, because I was worried that an article about Patricia might make her well-known and might take her away from me.

"I love you, Danielle," she says and she kisses me on the cheek. "You make me feel safe. London is good fun, but I'm so glad to be going home to our little house and our animals and our new orchard."

"So am I," I agree. "I guess we're not cut out to be rich and famous, just rich will suit us very nicely. Don't you agree?" I ask and she hugs me.

"Absolutely," she replies.

CHAPTER 49

I'm home, I'm home and I'm so relieved. I park the car outside our front gate and I feel so happy to be here. The familiarity of this place surrounds me and comforts me and I'm filled with love for it and all that it represents. Driving up from Gerona, I stared in wonder at the sky, which seemed bluer, and the mountains, which seemed greener than I remembered and the sun shone so brightly, I swear it has never been that bright before.

I've survived London. I didn't get lost in the busy streets and I didn't make a fool of myself with the upper classes and now I'm home, safe and sound. Anticipating our arrival Marjorie has put Ollee in the garden and, when the dog sees us, he goes berserk. He runs round and round, faster and faster until his back legs overtake his front legs and he trips himself up, rolls over a flowerpot, before ending up on his back in the herb garden.

"Are you coming in?" I ask him as I unlock the front door. The excited dog jumps to his feet and makes a bee-line for the opening. He manages to enter the house before either Patricia or me then he twirls around and barks at us, as if urging us to get a move on. I love my home but I hadn't realised just how much until I step through the door. It's as if Patricia and I have filled it, not only with our belongings, but also our hearts and our souls. The cat is lying on the arm of my chair and she stretches her legs and lifts her head when she sees me. I receive a brief look of acknowledgement then she resumes her sleep, what a contrast to the welcome given by Ollee I think, but how normal for the cat.

We quickly unpack our cases, and with Ollee in tow, Patricia and I head for town to eat dinner at one of the local restaurants. Not quite up to the glamour of Michel Albert's, but it suits us just fine and dining out just rounds off the holiday nicely. Everyone we meet wants to hear about our trip and we eventually roll home when it's dark, after consuming several glasses of wine. I'm actually looking forward to going into the office tomorrow and I don't know if it's because of the alcohol or simply the relief of being home.

When I wake in the morning I have a slight headache, probably too much wine last night, but the travelling also has made me unusually tired. Whatever the cause I take the precaution of donning my sunglasses before stepping out of the house into the early morning sunshine. It's a wise decision because the light is fantastic in the mountains, but the brightness won't help my hangover.

I enter the office and see that Paul and Laurent are already at their desks. The familiar smell of coffee reaches me and Paul jumps up to pour me a cup.

"Late night, Boss?" he asks pointing to my sunglasses. "You had a good time in London then," he adds with a wink.

I quickly remove my sunglasses which I'd forgotten I was wearing. "I had a great time in London,

Paul, thank you very much," I reply. "And no, I didn't have a late night."

"I'll bring your coffee over," he says. "Then I'll fill you in on one or two things that I think you'll want to know about. Okay?" he asks.

"I suppose so," I reply. Maybe being back in the office isn't as good as I'd anticipated.

He tells me there's still no sign of either Raymond Dupree or Raul Armin, but Madame Dupree has officially registered her son as a missing person and she's already telephoned this morning looking for an update. Detective Gerard has also been on the phone this morning, and he's jumping up and down, Paul's words not mine, about Raymond. He's furious he's still not been found. He doesn't care a bit about Raul, but to have a police officer listed as missing is simply not acceptable.

"Does he want me to call him back?" I ask. I feel sick at the thought.

"No," he replies. "I asked him and he said he doesn't want to hear from this office until Raymond is located. He also said he expects that to be within forty-eight hours, Boss."

"No pressure then," I say and he gives me a wry smile.

"What would you like me to do, Boss? Laurent and I have covered every place we think Raymond might go. He seems to have vanished off the face of the planet."

I remember my conversation with Phoebe, but I don't want to send my men on a wild goose chase, so I decide to wait and see, what, if anything occurs. All the police officers in the region are keeping an eye out for Raymond. Surely he has to turn up somewhere, sometime.

"We'll wait," I say to Paul. "And Detective Gerard will just have to be patient as well. If he phones again tell him I'm out and, if he insists on speaking to me, tell him I'm following a lead and can't be reached. That should give us a bit more time."

"And do you have a lead?" he asks.

"That's for me to know," I say. "You'll just have to be patient too."

CHAPTER 50

Wednesday comes and goes without incident which is just the way I like it. No more worrying phone calls or idiots asking stupid questions. There are very few tourists left in town and the number of 'curists' visiting the spa is beginning to dwindle. Everything is gradually getting back to normal.

Thursday is a typical autumn day except that it's intensely hot. There's still not a trace of Raymond Dupree and, as the morning progresses, I begin to feel edgy. I get a jag of fear every time the phone rings in case it's Detective Gerard. It's apparent to me now, that if someone doesn't wish to be found, it's quite easy for them to disappear. It goes some way to explaining why a large number of people who run away, never turn up, even with stringent searching.

By lunchtime, I can stand the pressure of the ringing phone no more. I call Patricia and arrange to meet her in the café for a bite to eat and, within twenty minutes, we're seated having a cold plate of Catalan salad and some home-made bread, all washed down with good strong Catalan beer. We are enjoying our food which is very good. Patricia has spread some paperwork pertaining to the order from Michel Albert on the table for me to look over for her and I'm just beginning to relax, when my mobile rings and it makes me jump.

I look at the number displayed on the screen, it's

familiar to me. I don't immediately recognise it, but at least I know it's not Detective Gerard's. I answer on the fourth ring and a familiar voice speaks.

"Hello, hello, are you there? It's me, Raymond."

I dive out of my seat practically tipping the table as I go and rush outside so I can get a better signal, and so I can take the call in private.

"Raymond," I hiss down the phone. "Where are you? Are you okay?"

"I'm fine, everything is fine now," he replies and I notice that his voice has a strange flatness about it.

"Where are you?" I repeat.

He sighs and he sounds tired, "I am in Le Perthus."

I immediately think about my conversation with Phoebe and her friend, and I wonder if Raymond has come into contact with Raul. I decide to take the softly, softly approach because I don't want to scare him into hanging up the phone.

"Can I meet with you? Can I help you," I ask gently. "You sound very tired Raymond."

"I am tired. I am so, so tired. It's the pills they gave me at the hospital and the pain killers. I just want to sleep."

"What's happened Raymond? Have you found Raul?"

"That bastard, he deserved to die. He killed her you know, he killed my Veronique."

"What have you done, Raymond? Are you in danger" I ask. I'm beginning to feel nervous.

Something is very wrong and I need to find Raymond quickly. As I'm talking, I run for my car. Patricia will understand if I don't come back into the restaurant and she'll pay the bill. With a bit of luck I'll be able to explain everything to her by the time I get home.

"I'm going to sit down because I'm very, very tired. I can't keep my eyes open," Raymond says. I notice his words have become slurred.

"Don't go to sleep, Raymond," I demand. "Stay awake, tell me where you are."

He gives me an address in Le Perthus and I fumble for my notebook and a pen. Then I manage to scribble it down.

"What's happened to Raul?" I ask "Speak to me, Raymond, tell me what you've done."

"He's dead. I killed him." His voice is very quiet and he sounds as if he can hardly speak with fatigue. "When he opened the door I stuck the screwdriver in his chest and he fell backwards. He's dead and I'm not sorry. I had to do it, I had to." His voice trails off.

I'm in my car now and I'm driving like a mad woman towards Le Perthus, but it will still take me about half an hour to get there.

"Stay awake, Raymond," I'm screaming down the phone, "Tell me about Veronique."

"She was beautiful," he says. Mentioning her name has done the trick, it revives him a bit.

"I had to get Raul for what he did. I had to get him before he had a chance to get me, so I stabbed him as soon as he opened the door. It was easy, so easy," his voice becomes weaker.

"Raymond, Raymond, talk to me." I demand.

"I had to avenge her death. I couldn't let him get away with what he'd done. Now I can join my darling girl. I miss her so much. I'm so empty without her." He begins to sob and his voice trails off again.

Oh God, I think, he's taken something, and that's why his voice sounds so tired and slurred. I don't want to hang up the phone and I can't phone for assistance while I'm speaking to him. I make the decision to keep him talking while I drive as fast as I can to reach him. Whether this is the right choice or the wrong choice, only time will tell.

CHAPTER 51

As I drive I feel sick and dazed because I'm so shocked by what's unfolding. I'm desperately trying to keep Raymond talking and I've almost reached the main street of Le Perthus when the line goes silent. I've driven at breakneck speed, but fortunately the winding road up the mountain to the frontier town is quiet, because of the time of year and the time of day. The main street is more Spanish looking than French and the border between the two countries is just at the end of this road. Le Perthus is full of glitzy shops selling designer wear, cheap cigarettes and alcohol, but these shops are all closed because it's lunchtime.

I park badly, abandon my car, and run towards the address I've been given. It's right on the corner of the main street so I find it easily. The front door is closed, before I touch the door handle I take latex gloves from my handbag and put them on. When I try the handle I find the door isn't locked and it swings open. Raul Armin is lying on his back in the hallway just as Raymond described to me.

When I enter the house the hallway is rather dark and narrow so I click on the light switch and push the door shut behind me. The hall is immediately bathed in a dull yellow light and, when I walk over to Raul, I see a large screwdriver is sticking out of his chest and he's covered in blood. His head is tilted backwards and his eyes are open. They seem to be staring at some spot on the wall behind his head. His face is contorted into a grimace. It's clear, from the way the blood is congealed, that he's been dead for some time.

I carefully step over his body and make my way through the house checking the rooms as I go and, when I enter the kitchen, I find Raymond sitting on the floor with his back to the wall. He's surrounded by empty pill bottles. I feel for a pulse in his neck to check whether I'm too late. Once I've confirmed he's dead all I can do is make a call to my colleagues and ask them to come and assist me then I search the house for evidence.

It takes quite a long time before anybody comes to my aid, but eventually two police officers do arrive, and I draw their attention to the kitchen sink where I point out the burnt remains of a notebook.

"I think this notebook is the key to both this murder and another one I'm investigating," I say. "I believe it has been a whore's client book although all that remains are the covers and some tiny fragments of paper. I'm involved in a major case, which is being overseen by Detective Gerard in Perpignan, so I'd be obliged if you could please call in forensics before you touch anything."

"We've been looking for this man for some time, Madame," one of the policemen says pointing to Raymond. "What led you here? How did you know that he'd be in Le Perthus?"

"I had a tip off," I say. "But I wasn't sure if it would be reliable, so it was more luck than planning."

I haven't told them the whole truth, but it's of no consequence now. I give them my card and tell them I'm the leading officer in both the murder, and the apparent suicide of Officer Dupree, and they must report to me. They're more than happy to agree. No one wants to take responsibility when the murderer is a police officer, even if he has conveniently committed suicide. I feel a mixture of elation and sadness. I'm sorry for Raymond's mother, because even though she's a selfish woman with little compassion, no mother should have to bury her son. I'm elated because I've solved the crimes and, once again, I'll come out of a major investigation looking good. When the paramedics and the doctor arrive I leave the scene and I walk back to my car. Exhaustion overwhelms me and I'm shaking with tiredness, so I sit in the driver's seat and rest my arms and my head on the steering wheel. After a minute or two, I take out my notebook, so I can plan exactly what to put in my report. It's important I cover every aspect of the case starting with the death of Madame Henriette which is looking more and more as if it could have been murder.

If I assume Raul had the client book in his possession when Raymond killed him, and Raymond found the book and subsequently burned it in the sink that ties up a loose end. Raul may or may not have obtained the book from Veronique or one of the other whores, but it makes no difference.

All of the men who attended the brothel of Madame Henriette will be relieved now the client book is destroyed. I can't wait to tell Marjorie that her husband's dirty little secret will never be discovered because I'm the only person who knows the truth. If I report, that in my opinion, Madame Henriette's death was indeed an unfortunate accident and that someone unknown took advantage of the situation by stealing the client book, then the case can be closed down. I've no doubt in my mind that Doctor Poullet will be happy to back up my conclusion. Michel Albert will be less upset at the thought of his mother dying accidentally, than being murdered.

There's no doubt Raul murdered Veronique and no doubt Raymond murdered Raul. However, I'll report that Raymond was not of sound mind when he committed the murder or when he took his own life. That will allow him a proper religious burial. I don't need to tell anyone I spoke to Raymond on the phone then I won't have to explain why I chose to drive to Le Perthus instead of immediately contacting the local police. It was my choice and maybe it was the wrong choice, but one can only do one's best. I shouldn't have to suffer any consequences for my decision.

I feel better now I've everything clear in my head. I've solved two murders and closed the case on an accidental death. No wonder the Commune Committee awarded me the 'Citizen of the Year' award. I deserved it. I wonder what accolades await me now. Detective Gerard better watch out because I might just have my sights on his job.

CHAPTER 52

It's been almost three weeks since the day I went to Le Perthus and everything has gone even better than I could have wished for. When I first returned to the office that day, Laurent barely lifted his head from his work and he moved about uncomfortably in his seat. Paul found it hard to meet my eyes and he refrained from his usual banter. When I asked them what was wrong Paul informed me Detective Gerard had phoned for an update and, as instructed, he told him I was unavailable as I was out of the office following a lead.

"He wants you to call him before end of day, Boss." Paul said.

He was completely unprepared for my response as the look of worry on his face made me burst into laughter. "Are you okay Boss?" he asked then he too began to laugh nervously. "Is your laughter from happiness or hysteria? I do hope it's happiness because Laurent is practically wetting his pants thinking you've gone nuts," he added.

"Would you like a coffee?" Laurent piped up. "And for the record, I'm not frightened, just concerned."

His response sets me off again. I think there's every chance that my laughter is from both happiness and hysteria.

"Yes, I would like a coffee Laurent, thank you very much." I replied, "And Paul, would you be so kind as to telephone Detective Gerard and apologise that I don't have the time to return his call personally, but assure him, that all outstanding business has been dealt with. You may also inform him a report will be on his desk by lunchtime tomorrow."

I was met with stunned silence and a look of admiration on their faces that I'll never ever forget. After that, the word about Madame Henriette's client book being found and burned in the dead man's flat, spread like wildfire, and for the next week I received all sorts of weird and wonderful gifts from some of the more remorseful men of the community. Everything from smoked ham to two live chickens arrived at the office. As if I needed any more chickens!

Raymond's funeral was held last week and it was very low key. It was thought that a police funeral would be inappropriate for a murderer, even if he was an officer of the law. His mother was only really interested in finding out how much money she'd get from his estate and I knew that whatever the sum, she'd never be satisfied.

Patricia and I are now the proud owners of the orchard and she and my father are getting on like a house on fire. It's wonderful to hear them chatting at the kitchen table and making plans. My mother still hasn't paid a visit to my house although she is frequently invited. However, she does now acknowledge me in the street instead of scuttling away and I'm thankful for small mercies.

I received a letter from Detective Gerard praising my exemplary police work and, although I was delighted with his kind words, I'd prefer more formal recognition, perhaps in the shape of a commendation. Still, I'm a patient woman and I have my sights on his job.

I'm sitting at the kitchen table chatting to Patricia when she begins asking me about my work. She tells me she's been talking to Marjorie.

"Marjorie said you helped her and saved her husband's career," she states. "She said you spoke to the brothel owner, Madame Henriette. I didn't know you visited Michel's mum before her death. How did you know her?"

I'm stunned she's asked me about this and I feel compelled to tell Patricia the truth about my involvement with Madame Henriette.

"I have something to tell you," I begin. "I haven't told you the whole truth about Madame Henriette. I haven't told anyone. What I say must remain between you and me. Nobody else must know. Can you keep my secret?"

Patricia looks worried, "You know you can tell me anything, anything at all. What's happened?" she asks. "You seem upset, Danielle."

I begin, "A few weeks ago Marjorie telephoned me in a blind panic. She said her husband had been visiting the house of Madame Henriette and that he'd told her all about it. She said he was distraught and begged her not to leave him. She also told me she'd forgiven him."

Patricia holds her hands over her mouth and her

eyes are wide with shock.

"But they're such a loving couple and they have children. How could he betray her like that?" she asks.

"Nobody really knows what goes on in other people's houses," I reply. "Anyway, she was very upset. She told me Madame Henriette had a client book and her husband had found out from one of the girls, that she was using it to extort money from some of her customers. The girl also told him that her boyfriend had asked her to steal the book. Naturally, the Mayor would have been an easy and lucrative target. Marjorie begged me to intervene. She asked me to try and get the client book from Madame Henriette before it fell into the wrong hands."

"Is that where Raul Armin comes in?" she asks.

"Well yes, he was certainly an unsavoury character and he could have done a lot of damage with the book. My plan was to visit Madame Henriette, threaten to keep charging her girls with prostitution and her with living off immoral earnings unless she gave me the book, but things didn't quite go to plan."

I walk over to the bureau and lift a bottle of wine then pour us both a glass.

"I waited outside her house until I saw her girls leave for the night then I knocked on the door. She called to me to come in and said the door was unlocked. I suppose she must have thought it was one of girls returning for something she'd forgotten. I went into the house and I could hear her in the kitchen so I entered the room. I could see she was surprised to see me."

I stop to take a deep drink of my wine and

Patricia takes her hands from her mouth and does the same.

"She asked me what I wanted and I told her I knew about the client book and then I made my threat to her. She laughed in my face. She held the book in her hand and taunted me with it. She said she was going to expose everyone in it to a national newspaper and they were going to pay her a fortune."

"Oh God, how awful," Patricia says. "What did you do?"

"I was blazing that the old whore would do such a thing and I made a grab for the book, I was determined to have it. Madame Henriette turned from me with the book in her hand. She tried to hold it out of my reach, but as she moved away from me, her foot caught on the leg of a chair and she tripped and fell through the window of the door. The glass severed an artery in her neck and she died instantly."

"Oh my God, Danielle. How terrible for you to witness such a thing. Whatever did you do next?"

"I grabbed the book and ran. I didn't know what else to do, Madame Henriette was dead, I couldn't help her, but I could help the poor souls who were named in the book."

"But how did the book turn up burnt in the sink of the house in Le Perthus?"

"When I arrived there both men were dead. I simply took the book from my bag and burned it before the local police arrived on the scene."

"How clever of you, Danielle, your quick thinking has saved our friends. How difficult it must have been for you to keep that ghastly secret for so long. Don't worry about a thing, my Darling. Everything will be fine now. I'm so proud of the way you've handled this. We need never speak of it again. I hope that by unburdening yourself to me, you'll be able to put it behind you and forget this terrible thing."

My dear Patricia can always put things into perspective. She always understands me and the things I have to do in my job. We finish our wine and we take Ollee for a walk and, while we walk, we plan how to invest my lottery winnings. How lucky I am, I think, my life is truly wonderful.

CHAPTER 53

ANOTHER TRUTH

I love the truth. There's a saying, 'the truth shall set you free' and I believe that, I really do. I told Patricia a truth and she loved me for it, she comforted me and she set my conscience free. It was not the whole truth, but I can live with that.

Let me tell you my story so you will understand how I feel and how I think. I entered the house of Madame Henriette and she was very surprised to see me. She was angry that I knew about her client book and, when I threatened her, she laughed in my face. She taunted me and told me she knew all about Patricia and me and our relationship, but that didn't anger me because our relationship is a loving friendship nothing more. What truly enraged me was when she threatened to make up lies about my darling girl and write them in her book.

"How tough will you be when your girlfriend's name is in my book?" she said "How dare you try to threaten me. I'll tell the world that your beloved girlfriend visited my whores. Two can play your game. You threaten me and I'll come back at you twice as bad."

In that instant I hated her and I wanted her dead. I think she realised she'd gone too far when I came at her in a blind fury. She tried to turn away, but I grabbed her by her over dyed hair and I pushed her head through the glass of the back door window. It shattered and the broken shards severed an artery in her neck. She died almost instantly. I don't regret killing Madame Henriette and I told Patricia most of the truth, so that's okay. I couldn't hurt her with the whole truth, could I?

Raymond Dupree, now there's another story. As soon as he telephoned me I knew exactly what I wanted to do. The client book had been in my handbag for weeks and, when Raymond told me he'd killed Raul, everything fell into place. When Raymond mentioned the pills from the hospital and the pain killers, then said Raul was dead and he could now join his beloved Veronique, I knew he'd taken an overdose. I hoped he'd taken an overdose.

I kept him talking on the phone so he couldn't change his mind and phone for help, and I felt safe when he stopped talking because I knew he'd passed out. When I arrived at the house of Raul Armin I put on latex gloves because I didn't want to leave my prints anywhere. Besides, it made it easier for me to finish off Raymond.

When I felt his neck for a pulse there was a very shallow beat so I covered Raymond's mouth and nose with my gloved hand. He put up no resistance because he was already unconscious. It only took a couple of minutes for him to die. I couldn't have him survive and tell everyone that I'd burned the book in the sink. He could never return to work because he was mad and his mother didn't want him back, so he had no future. I was helping him along, that's all. He wanted to die. I simply helped him along.

#####

A Message from Danielle

Thank you for reading 'Red Light in the Pyrenees. I do hope you enjoyed it.

You know me much better now and I think you like me, even with my dark secrets. Sometimes crime does pay.

If you would like to know more about me, and the place where I live, then you now have further opportunity.

Also written by Elly Grant and published by Author Way Limited are 'Dead End in the Pyrenees' and 'Deadly Degrees in the Pyrenees' Also, if you haven't already seen them, you may like 'Palm Trees in the Pyrenees.' And 'Grass Grows in the Pyrenees'

Till soon
Danielle

Other books by Elly Grant –
From the Death in the Pyrenees series

'Palm Trees in the Pyrenees' is the first book in Elly Grant's series 'Death in the Pyrenees'. The story unfolds, told by Danielle a single, downtrodden , thirty year old, who is the only cop in the small Pyrenean town. She feels unappreciated and unnoticed, having been passed over for promotion in favour of her male colleagues working in the region. But everything is about to change. The sudden and mysterious death of a much hated locally based Englishman will have far reaching affects.

'Grass Grows in the Pyrenees' is the second book in Elly Grant's series 'Death in the Pyrenees'. The story unfolds, told by Danielle, a single, thirty year old, recently promoted cop. The sudden and mysterious death of a local farmer suspected of growing cannabis, opens a 'Pandora's' box of trouble. It's a race against time to stop the gangsters before the town, and everyone in it, is damaged beyond repair

'Dead End in the Pyrenees' is the fourth book in Elly Grant's series 'Death in the Pyrenees'.

The story unfolds, told by Danielle, a single, thirty-something, highly-respected, female cop. A sudden and unexpected death at the local spa brings to light other mysterious deaths. Important local people are involved, people who Danielle respects. She must quickly solve the case before things get out of control

'Deadly Degrees in the Pyrenees' is the fifth book in Elly Grant's series 'Death in the Pyrenees'.

The story unfolds, told by Danielle, a single, thirty-something, senior, female cop. The ghastly murder of a local estate agent reveals unscrupulous business deals. Danielle's friends may be in danger. She must catch the killer before anyone else is harmed

All these stories are about life in a small French town, local events, colourful characters, prejudice and of course, death.

Elly Grant

Chapter 1 of 'Dead End in the Pyrenees'

The blow to his head wasn't hard enough to render Monsieur Dupont unconscious but it stupefied him. Blood poured profusely from a deep scalp wound down into his left eye. He flopped onto the recently washed tiles at the side of the Roman bath then floundered at the edge, frantically trying to stop his body from slipping completely into the pool. His upper torso overhung the edge, his hands slapping at the water as he tried to right himself. He was aware of the metal chair, which was attached to a hoist to enable the disabled to enter the water, beginning to descend. As it lowered it trapped Monsieur Dupont, forcing his head and shoulders under the water. He struggled, his toes drumming the moist tiles, his arms making a flapping motion, but he was hopelessly stuck. Soon he succumbed. Brimstone smelling steam rose from the surface of the spa pool and silence returned.

When Madame Georges arrived for work she was surprised to hear a low, electronic, whirring sound coming from the pool area. She couldn't think what it was. Surely the machinery and gadgets, designed to treat all manner of ailments, had been switched off at the close of business the night before. The last treatments were usually completed by 7pm then everyone went home leaving Monsieur Dupont, the caretaker, to lock up.

Following the sound, Madame Georges entered the majestic Roman spa. The double doors swung silently closed behind her as she made her way towards the pool. She was aware of her feet, still encased in outdoor shoes, making a slapping sound on the tiled floor. Madame Georges immediately noticed that the hoist chair was down and something was bundled up beneath it at the water's edge, but as her spectacles were steamed-up from the damp atmosphere, she couldn't tell what that something was until she was practically on top of it.

"Oh, mon Dieu," she said aloud on realising that what had looked like a bundle of rags, was in fact, a man.

A wave of shock passed through her body, she took off her glasses with shaking hands, cleaned them on the hem of her blouse then stared again. It was definitely a man. His body was still and there was what seemed to be blood, gathered in a puddle on the tiles beneath it. Madame Georges did not immediately recognise the person as the head and shoulders were under water. All the staff at 'les thermes' wore pink track-suits and trainers to work, and the guests were usually attired in white, towelling, dressing gowns and blue, rubber, pool shoes. This person was clothed in a dark-coloured suit and had formal shoes on his feet.

Regaining some of her composure, Madame Georges turned and ran back through the double, swing doors towards the office. She used her key to let herself in then immediately pressed the button to sound the alarm. The alarm was a wartime relic, a former air-raid siren, still used to alert people to an emergency. It wailed out over the valley and across the mountains twice. People who would normally have gone back to sleep at the first blast were now fully awake. The queue of chattering shoppers, waiting in line at the 'boulangerie' to buy their baguettes, fell silent, each person straining to listen for approaching emergency vehicles. This double call was used only for the most serious of incidents.

Madame Georges sank into a chair then she picked up the phone and dialled the emergency number to report what she'd discovered.

"Oh, mon Dieu, mon Dieu, a man is dead. I'm sure he is dead. There has been an accident, I think. Assistance, s'il vous plait, please come at once, please help me, I am alone here," she said, when her call was answered. Madame Georges had seen death before many times. The spa attracted the sick and the old searching for cures for various ailments and many of them spent the last days of their lives there, but this was different.

Like a well-oiled machine, everything flowed into action. Before very long the 'pompiers', who are firemen and trained paramedics arrived, along with an ambulance and a local practitioner named Doctor Poullet. A crowd began to gather in the street outside. But prior to this whole circus kicking off, I was the first on the scene accompanied by one of my trainee officers. We managed to calm down Madame Georges before securing the area and this is where my story begins.

Also by Elly Grant

The Unravelling of Thomas Malone

The mutilated corpse of a young prostitute is discovered in a squalid apartment.

Angela Murphy has recently started working as a detective on the mean streets of Glasgow. Just days into the job she's called to attend this grisly murder. She is shocked by the horror of the scene. It's a ghastly sight of blood and despair.

To her boss, Frank Martin, there's something horribly familiar about the scene.

Is this the work of a copycat killer?

Will he strike again?

With limited resources and practically no experience, Angela is desperate to prove herself.

But is her enthusiasm sufficient?

Can she succeed before the killer strikes again?

Never Ever Leave Me

Katy Bradley had a perfect life, or so she thought. Perfect husband, perfect job and a perfect home until one day, one awful day when everything fell apart. Full of fear and dread, Katy had no choice but to run, but would her split second decision carry her forward to safety or back to the depths of despair? A chance encounter with a handsome stranger gives her hope. Never ever leave me, sees Katy trapped between two worlds, her future and her past. Will she have the strength to survive? Will she ever find happiness again?

Released by Elly Grant Together with Angi Fox

But Billy Can't Fly

At over six feet tall, blonde and blue-eyed, Billy looks like an Adonis, but he is simple minded, not the full shilling, one slice less than a sandwich, not quite right in the head. When you meet him you might not notice at first, but after a couple of minutes it becomes apparent. The lights are on but nobody's home. In Billy's mind, he's Superman, a righter of wrongs, a saver of souls and that's where it all goes wrong. He interacts with the people he meets at a bus stop, Jez, a rich public schoolboy, Melanie the office slut, Bella Worthington, the leader of the local W.I. and David, a gay, Jewish teacher. This book moves quickly along as each character tells their part of the tale. Billy's story is darkly funny, poignant and tragic. Full of stereotypical prejudices, it offends on every level, but is difficult to put down.

Released by Elly Grant Together with Zach Abrams

Twists and Turns

With fear, horror, death and despair, these stories will surprise you, scare you and occasionally make you smile. Twists & Turns offer the reader thought provoking tales. Whether you have a minute to spare or an hour or more, open Twists & Turns for a world full of mystery, murder, revenge and intrigue. A unique collaboration by the authors Elly Grant and Zach Abrams

About the author

Hi, my name is Elly Grant and I like to kill people. I use a variety of methods. Some I drop from a great height, others I drown, but I've nothing against suffocation, poisoning or simply battering a person to death. As long as it grabs my reader's attention, I'm satisfied.

I've written several novels and short stories. My first novel, 'Palm Trees in the Pyrenees' is set in a small town in France. It is published by Author Way Limited. Author Way has already published the next three novels in the series, 'Grass Grows in the Pyrenees,' 'Red Light in the Pyrenees' and 'Dead End in the Pyrenees' as well as a collaboration of short stories called 'Twists and Turns'.

As I live in a small French town in the Eastern Pyrenees, I get inspiration from the way of life and the colourful characters I come across. I don't have to search very hard to find things to write about and living in the most prolific wine producing region in France makes the task so much more delightful.

When I first arrived in this region I was lulled by the gentle pace of life, the friendliness of the people and the simple charm of the place. But dig below the surface and, like people and places the world over, the truth begins to emerge. Petty squabbles, prejudice, jealousy and greed are all there waiting to be discovered. Oh, and what joy in that discovery. So, as I sit in a café, or stroll by the riverside, or walk high into the mountains in the sunshine I greet everyone I meet with a smile and a 'Bonjour' and, being a friendly place, they return the greeting. I people watch as I sip my wine or when I go to buy my baguette. I discover quirkiness and quaintness around every corner. I try to imagine whether the subjects of my scrutiny are nice or nasty and, once I've decided, some of those unsuspecting people, a very select few, I kill.

Perhaps you will visit my town one day. Perhaps you will sit near me in a café or return my smile as I walk past you in the street. Perhaps you will hold my interest for a while, and maybe, just maybe, you will be my next victim. But don't concern yourself too much, because, at least for the time being, I always manage to confine my murderous ways to paper.

Read books from the 'Death in the Pyrenees' series, enter my small French town and meet some of the people who live there ----- and die there.

To contact the author
mailto:ellygrant@authorway.net

About Author Way Limited

Author Way provides a broad range of good quality, previously unpublished works and makes them available to the public on multiple formats.

We have a fast growing number of authors who have completed or are in the process of completing their books and preparing them for publication and these will shortly be available.

Please keep checking our website to hear about the latest developments.

Author Way Limited

www.authorway.net

Made in the USA
Charleston, SC
28 August 2013